*A
Harlequin
Romance*

THE HEAD OF THE HOUSE

by

MARGARET MALCOLM

HARLEQUIN BOOKS

Toronto • Canada   New York • New York

THE HEAD OF THE HOUSE

First published in 1969 by Mills & Boon, Limited,
17-19 Foley Street, London, England.

Harlequin Canadian edition published April, 1971
Harlequin U.S. edition published July, 1971

The Harlequin trade mark, consisting of the
word HARLEQUIN® and the portrayal of a
Harlequin, is registered in the United States Patent
Office and in the Canada Trade Marks Office.

Standard Book Number: 373-51488-3.

Printed in Canada

CHAPTER I

THE message was brought to Eleanor just as she was finishing her solitary breakfast.

"Mr. Simon would be obliged, Miss Eleanor, if you'd come to his study before leaving for the works."

"Yes, of course, Manning," Eleanor promised cheerfully without making any attempt to find out why her Uncle Simon should want to see her now in view of the fact that she had expected that, as usual, she would be driving him to the famous Chalfont pottery works which he controlled. "Will you tell Mr. Simon that I'll be up in under five minutes?"

Manning, Simon Chalfont's personal attendant, bowed slightly and made his way out of the room in that deliberate and dignified manner which some members of the Chalfont family found so irritating.

Eleanor finished her meal, went along the corridor to her bedroom and from a drawer which she kept locked, took out a notebook and a key. She was going back along the corridor when she heard her mother call rather fretfully from her bedroom.

Eleanor opened the door and put her head in.

"Hallo, darling, anything wrong?" she asked affectionately.

"Oh no, nothing wrong—unless, of course, you think it's at all important that I've hardly had a minute's sleep all night," her mother replied plaintively.

At forty-three, Kitty Chalfont was still a pretty woman, but the discontent she made no attempt to hide was beginning to mar her fair, fragile beauty. What had once been an occasional and charmingly provocative pout had now developed into a permanent habit, and even a weekly massage could not wipe out the pucker between her skilfully shaped eyebrows.

The trouble was that Kitty Chalfont was quite sure life had treated her unfairly. At eighteen, just beginning to make her way as a professional ballroom dancer, she had been involved in a motor accident. It wasn't a very serious one, but Kitty's right ankle was injured. In time she was able to walk without a limp, but her dancing days were over. Never very thrifty by nature, Kitty had rapidly come to the end of what little money she had, and could see no way of earning any more. She had really enjoyed dancing and had worked hard to become successful, but she had no illusions about herself. Anything requiring mental effort was completely beyond her, and in any case, she had no money to pay for training of any sort.

It was at this point, when she was as nearly desperate as such a feather-brained little person could be, that she met Roger Chalfont, then in his early forties. He fell deeply in love with her, and though Kitty's feeling for him was no more than a blend of relief and gratitude for having rescued her from her plight, it was a reasonably happy marriage. Eleanor was born a year later, when Kitty was nineteen. It wasn't, perhaps, a very exciting life for a girl who had loved the limelight, but she was too shrewd not to appreciate the security she had found with Roger. Besides, there were bright spots. Roger did most of the travelling for the firm, and Kitty had gone all over the world with him, thoroughly enjoying the admiration her beauty evoked.

Then, when Kitty was twenty-eight and Eleanor nine, Roger died, leaving her not very well off. It was true that the family, which meant Roger's father and later, his brother Simon, made her an allowance, but it wasn't the same. No more trips abroad, no more excuse to buy masses of pretty clothes—Kitty was bored and discontented. Worse than that, she was worried. Attractive she might still be, but time was getting on. Heavens, how it was getting on! Why, Eleanor was nearly twenty-four—

"Poor darling," Eleanor said gently, feeling guilty because her own night had been one of healthy, dreamless sleep. "Is there anything I can do?"

"There might be—if you didn't spend so much of your time at those grimy works," Kitty grumbled. And then, as Eleanor didn't reply, she went on reproachfully: "I believe you'd have gone off without coming to see me if I hadn't called to you!"

"No, I'd have come," Eleanor assured her. "Only Uncle Simon wants to see me before I leave—"

"Simon does?" The information so surprised Mrs. Chalfont that she sat up in bed quite energetically. "But what on earth for? Isn't he going to the office today?"

"I've no idea," Eleanor told her, thankful that she was able to say that quite truthfully. It wasn't always easy to combine the duties of a daughter and of her uncle's confidential secretary. "Manning just brought me the message—"

"Manning!" Kitty said impatiently. "That man annoys me! Always looking down that long nose of his as if he thinks no one's as good as he is!"

Eleanor didn't answer. She never quite knew what to say when her mother was in this sort of mood, and it made her all the more unhappy because it emphasised the gulf that against her will she had to acknowledge was growing wider all the time.

Perhaps Kitty sensed something of what her daughter was feeling, and certainly because, despite the somewhat shallowness of her nature, she was really fond of Eleanor, she stretched out a placatory hand towards her.

"Darling, I'm being naughty, aren't I?" she apologised with a deprecatory little grimace. "And I've really no excuse except—oh well, never mind that either. Pop along and see Simon and then, if you've a minute, come back to me, will you? There's something I want—" once again she broke off. "Off you go!"

At least partially reassured, Eleanor withdrew her head and shut the door of her mother's room. Partway along the corridor, she turned a corner into a small hall whose heavy mahogany door looked disproportionately large in that setting. Eleanor let herself out and walked along the covered arcade which led to the house proper.

Kingsworthy House had been built some hundred and seventy-five years earlier, the latest of the homes which had been built on the same site over the centuries. It was a not very good specimen of Palladian architecture, the main part of the house being overburdened with badly proportioned columns and a pediment which looked too heavy for their spindly support. On either side of the house was a covered way supported by still more columns leading in each case to a pavilion. It was in one of these that Eleanor and her mother lived. The other was the home of Mr. and Mrs. Edgar Chalfont and their two children, Celia and Dick.

Even so early the big front door stood open as if to welcome Eleanor, but in fact it was because the ground floor had been turned into a museum. It had, perhaps, been a somewhat vainglorious act on the part of Eleanor's grandfather, for the exhibits dealt exclusively with the development of the Chalfont potteries from very small beginnings with specimens of the work done by them. None the less, the display was of considerable historical interest, for Simon and Edgar were the fourth generation from the Chalfont who had founded the firm in the eighteenth century—by a coincidence in the same year that the Tudor Kingsworthy House had been burnt down and the building of the present one commenced.

At the back of the hall a staircase rose in a lovely curve—it was, in fact, the best piece of design in the whole house. Eleanor went up this, along a short corridor and so to a door which had been added so that the upper rooms were completely cut off from the ground floor. Here Simon lived in a privacy which he valued more than any other of his possessions—and he was a rich man. Only Eleanor, since she had become his secretary, had a key to that door, and it had been made very clear not only to her but to all the other members of the family that it was to be used by her only when she came on business, and must be neither lent nor borrowed in any circumstances.

Simon was sitting at the big desk in his study when Eleanor went in. He greeted her with a brief nod and came straight to the point.

"I'm expecting a telephone call some time during the morning," he told her crisply. "If it comes through while you're here, you'll please go downstairs immediately. Understand?"

"Yes, Uncle Simon." Eleanor was completely unperturbed by the abruptness of his manner and the fact that she was to be dismissed so summarily.

A faintly sardonic smile touched his thin lips.

"Not in the least curious to know why I'm making such a mystery of it?" he asked quizzically.

Eleanor laughed—a very pretty soft laugh that expressed genuine amusement.

"Of course I am!" she said frankly. "I wouldn't be human if I wasn't, now would I?"

"Perhaps not," he agreed. "But I gather you don't resent me wanting to keep my own counsel?"

"No, I don't," Eleanor replied unhesitatingly. "In fact, I rather envy your ability to do it." And unconsciously, she sighed.

"H'm!" Simon gave her a shrewd look. "Which means *you* aren't always able to. That it?"

"Perhaps," Eleanor admitted reluctantly.

"H'm!" Simon said again, and passed his hand thoughtfully over his neat white Vandyke beard. "Does that mean you agree with your Aunt Helen? Don't think it's wise to have all the family under one roof?"

"Well, we're not really under the same roof, are we?" Eleanor answered evasively. "Really, the two pavilions are quite separate from the house and each other, aren't they?"

"True," Simon agreed, not seeming to think it worth while pressing the point. Instead, he took her left hand in his and gently touched the pretty ring that sparkled there. "Tell me, Eleanor, just what do you and young Baynes intend to do when you get married? That's in three months' time, isn't it?"

"Yes, at the end of August," Eleanor replied. "What do you mean, Uncle? Geoff will carry on with his riding school—"

"So I had supposed, since it's his only means of earning a livelihood," Simon said with a dryness that brought a flush to Eleanor's cheeks and made her pull her hand from his. "What I had really meant is, do you intend to share what is really only a bachelor flat over the stables or are you planning something different?"

"Well, that rather depends," Eleanor said hesitantly.

"On—?"

"Well, on whether I keep on working or not," she explained.

Simon shook his head.

"Not as my secretary, my dear," he said firmly. "I'm sorry, but much as I'd regret losing you, I don't think that as a young married woman you could give me the undivided loyalty that I am of the opinion your job requires."

"But, Uncle—" Eleanor protested.

"I know, my dear, I know," he interrupted. "You're going to tell me that it wouldn't make any difference. Well, I believe that in fairness to your husband-to-be, it ought to. Marriage is a very tricky business, and don't tell me that because I'm a bachelor I'm not qualified to give an opinion. Lookers on, you know! And I'd much rather your marriage didn't go on the rocks because of anything even remotely connected with me. I'm very fond of you, child, and I'm truly concerned for your happiness. Now then—to business. Got your notebook? Good! Well—"

He dictated several letters, gave instructions that she was to pass on as soon as she reached the office. Then they were interrupted by the ringing of the telephone bell. Eleanor promptly stood up, but was waved back to her chair.

"Only the house phone," Simon said as he lifted it. "Yes?"

A woman's voice, unpleasantly resonant and strident, answered him. Wincing slightly, Simon held the instrument an inch or so from his ear. With his head resting on his other hand he closed his eyes as he listened. He looked very tired, Eleanor thought sympathetically, which didn't surprise her, for she knew perfectly well who it was speaking. Aunt Alice, Uncle Edgar's wife. No one else had a voice like that—and no one else had such a gift for tiring people who came in contact with her!

"No, I'm sorry, Alice, I can't see you now. Yes, I shall be a little late going to the office, but that's because I'm expecting a private and confidential telephone call. As soon as that comes through, I shall be leaving. In any case—" he hesitated momentarily, glancing at Eleanor's dark, downbent head, "if you're thinking of continuing the conversation we had last night, then you're just wasting your time! I made it

THE HEAD OF THE HOUSE

perfectly clear—yes, I know all that, but I've told you
how I feel about it, and I haven't changed my mind.
Now you must excuse me, Alice—" and very firmly, he
hung up.

But the thread of his thoughts had been broken and
with an impatient gesture he indicated that Eleanor
could go.

"That woman—" he said irritably. "To be quite
honest, Eleanor, I've never yet met a woman who didn't
annoy me at some time or other, but Alice—well, it's
all the time! How the devil Edgar puts up with her I
don't know, and still less how it was that he ever came
to marry her!"

It was something about which Eleanor had often
puzzled. Aunt Alice, so self-opinionated, so incapable
of seeing any other point of view than her own, and
Uncle Edgar, gentle and kindly, an artist to his finger
tips and as completely unassuming as if he was not
brilliant in his own particular line. What made Eleanor
feel so bad, however, was the fact that Aunt Alice
made no attempt to disguise the fact that she despised
her husband. That, she felt, was quite horrible.

"Uncle, why do people make such awful mistakes?"
she asked impulsively. "I mean, Uncle Edgar must
always have been sensitive and—and retiring—"

"Just so," Simon agreed. "And Alice always had a
ruthless, aggressive streak in her. But there is such a
thing as the attraction of opposites. Edgar has always
felt himself to be ineffectual. Consequently he feels—
or used to feel—that decisiveness in other people is an
admirable quality. Alice—I've never been really sure
what prompted her to marry Edgar. In some women, it
might have been that his diffidence made an appeal to
her maternal instincts. But though I may be doing her
an injustice, I can't quite see Alice—Helen, of course,
has no doubts on the matter and makes no bones about
saying so. In her opinion, Alice is the domineering type
and naturally chose a man she thought she'd be able to
push about. But of course she's found she can't do that.
She's the ambitious type, but to Edgar the ambitions
that spur most men on mean absolutely nothing. And
that's that. It's not obstinacy on Edgar's part. It's simply

a matter of it being his nature and he *can't* change, whether he'd like to or not."

"I don't think he does want to," Eleanor said slowly, and Simon, mild surprise in his eyes, nodded.

"Very perceptive of you, child," he approved. "He doesn't. So he's developed a sort of protective shell he can crawl into, which makes Alice all the more aggressive, which makes Edgar—" He shrugged his shoulders. "An increasingly vicious circle! Do you wonder I've remained a bachelor?"

Eleanor stared blankly out of the window. The grounds of Kingsworthy House were famous for their beauty and had never looked more lovely than now when they were flaming with masses of rhododendrons. The grass was brilliantly green in silky swathes and the sun was shining. Yet it seemed to Eleanor that some of the pearly beauty of the May morning had gone. Involuntarily she shivered.

At that moment the telephone bell rang, and rather thankfully Eleanor made her escape. She walked slowly down the wide staircase and so back to the West Pavilion and her mother's room.

Kitty was up now and was sitting at her dressing table, putting on her make-up.

"Though why on earth I worry, I can't think," she grumbled. "There's nobody to notice—what did Simon want?"

"Just to dictate some letters and notes because he's not ready to go to the office yet," Eleanor explained.

Kitty half turned, her blue eyes alert.

"Not ready? But why? He's not ill, is he?"

"Oh no, nothing like that," Eleanor told her quickly. "Just he's waiting for a phone call to come through."

"Is he, though?" Kitty's eyes narrowed speculatively. "Then it must be something he doesn't want anyone to know about, because his line is completely independent of any other to the house—which I imagine isn't true of his office line?"

"No, it isn't," Eleanor admitted unwillingly.

"I suppose he didn't give you a hint—?" Kitty suggested pensively.

"No, he didn't," Eleanor said bluntly.

"And you wouldn't tell me if he had," Kitty said with good-humoured resignation. "Quite right, of course. I was only curious because of something I overheard at the hairdresser's yesterday. The woman in the next cubicle told her assistant that she'd heard Chalfont's and Stapleton's were amalgamating or one taking the other over or something—" she cocked an enquiring eye at her daughter.

"Absolute nonsense!" Eleanor declared robustly. "Stapleton's, of all firms! Why, they've been our biggest rivals for at least fifty years. At least, not exactly rivals because what they turn out isn't nearly so good as what we do. But they're always trying to steal our markets by undercutting our price, which of course they can afford to do because they're offering an inferior article."

"I wonder if they are, really?" Kitty meditated. "Or whether it's just Simon's prejudice?"

"I'm sure it isn't," Eleanor insisted. "We offer an honest job for an honest price—Stapleton's—"

"Oh, all right, all right, forget it!" Kitty waved a dismissive hand. Then she grimaced rather wryly. "You're an absolute Chalfont, aren't you, Eleanor? I sometimes find it astonishing to think that I contributed anything at all to your arrival in this world! There's certainly no sign of it—unless, perhaps, that you've got nice flat ears. That's something to be thankful for, anyway. Your poor father's were rather prominent."

"Mother!" Eleanor protested laughingly.

"Oh, I know, darling, quite shocking! Speak no ill of the dead and all that. None the less, prominent ears aren't exactly prepossessing, particularly in a girl, so let me take that little bit of comfort to myself! And now hadn't you better be off, or Chalfont or not, you'll be getting your cards!"

"But I thought there was something you wanted to say to me," Eleanor reminded her.

"There was. About Stapleton's. That was all," Kitty explained.

"Oh—well, then I'll go—"

This time, on leaving the West Pavilion, Eleanor made her way round to the back of the house where the

stables were and the old coach house over which
Geoffrey Baynes had his bachelor flat.

He had already run Eleanor's little car out from the
coach-house into the yard and was now sitting on the
old stone mounting block, reading the morning paper.
He stood up when he heard Eleanor's footsteps on the
cobbles, and smiled at her as he folded the paper.

Eleanor's heart turned over. She had known Geoff
all her life and had fallen in love with him when she was
about nine and he was some four or five years older. She
had followed him around like a little dog, despite dis-
couragement. Then, for years, they had seen little of
one another since both had been at boarding schools
while during the long summer holidays, Eleanor had
spent most of the time at the seaside while Geoff, less
fortunate than she, had spent them in the little village
house where he lived with his widowed mother.

To Eleanor, he had always been a romantic figure.
Not only had he always been well built and extremely
handsome in a fair, Scandinavian way, but he was also
that luckless character, usually of fiction, the heir who
had lost his inheritance.

For there had been a time when it was the Baynes
family who lived at Kingsworthy House—who had, in
fact, built this latest version of it. But while the Chalfonts had been gradually coming up in the world, the
Baynes had been as steadily losing the ability to support
any sort of social position and had at last had to sell
their home. Bad luck—bad management? Geoff would
shrug his shoulders if the question was put to him. After
all, what did the reason matter? That's how things were,
and making a fuss and having a post-mortem wouldn't
make any difference. Even when, by an ironical twist of
fate, he returned to Kingsworthy House to run his riding stables and live in accommodation that his several
times great-grandfather's grooms had occupied, he
seemed to find the situation amusing.

Geoff was, in fact, a very easy-going young man. So
long as he could pay his way and have a little bit left
over to spend on his really very modest pleasures, the
sun shone so far as he was concerned. As he put it
"Life's for living, not for slogging so that you come to

the end of it before you've found time to enjoy yourself." Which was, of course, entirely his own affair so long as he didn't ask anyone to share his life. And, realising that, he had hesitated before asking Eleanor to marry him. But after all, things always did turn out all right for him. Why, dash it, look at the way he'd just won over a hundred on that rank outsider he'd been tipped! If that, coming at such a moment, didn't mean that he was to buy a really decent ring for Eleanor, what could it mean?

So for three months his ring had sparkled on her finger and in another three months they planned to be married. And if nothing turned up to enable them to make a very spectacular start in life, did it really matter? They were young and healthy, the riding school was doing increasingly well, and of course, Eleanor would go on working for a time—

Only now she knew she wouldn't be able to do that. Her heart sank in the face of his cheerful welcome. How on earth was she going to tell him what Uncle Simon had just said? It was going to upset all their plans.

The stable clock chimed the half hour and with relief, Eleanor realised that she'd have to put off telling him until later, or else she would be so late getting to work that Uncle Simon's messages would have lost their point.

All the same, she let him detain her a few minutes. How could she help it when, after she had got into the little car, he leant his arms on the edge of the car window and smiled down admiringly at her.

"I like you in those crisp little outfits you wear for the office," he told her. "You ought always to wear plain things, Eleanor. They suit you."

"Plain clothes for a plain Jane?" Eleanor suggested mischievously.

"Plain Jane nothing!" Geoff declared vigorously. "But clean-cut and unfussy, yes! And don't fish for compliments, young woman, or you may get more than you bargain for!"

She patted his hand and smiled, her worries temporarily forgotten because it was just about impossible to be depressed in Geoff's company. Then, quite suddenly, he said something which banished that sense of well-being in a single breath.

"Eleanor, is there anything in this story about Chalfont's and Stapleton's merging?"

She stared at him speechlessly for a moment.

"Where on earth did *you* get hold of that story?" she demanded.

"At the local," he explained. "So it's true—but still supposed to be on the secret list. Is that it?"

"No, it isn't," Eleanor declared energetically. "It was just that I was surprised because you're the second person who's asked me that this morning—the other one was Mother. She heard it at the hairdresser's. And it's such absolute nonsense. I simply can't think what's started such a story."

Geoff shrugged his shoulders.

"Well, you should know, if anyone does," he commented. "But I can tell you this—something happened last weekend while you and your mother were up in town that suggested to me there was something in it."

"What?" Eleanor asked sharply.

"Young Stapleton dined here on Saturday evening," Geoff explained. "And that's not just hearsay. I saw him with my own eyes. Spoke to him as well, in fact. He drove that flashy car of his into this yard and asked if it would be all right to park it for an hour or so while he was having dinner here."

"What an extraordinary thing," Eleanor said slowly. "All the same, I don't think it's really confirmation that the story's true. Much more likely that he came for some totally different reason and it was what sparked off the rumour. He may even have been dining with Uncle Edgar. And now I really must go, Geoff. See you this evening."

She drove competently out of the yard, along the wide gravel drive and so through the big gates and out into the road. For perhaps half a mile the road ran through farm land. Then came pleasant, well-spaced houses of the older type. But gradually the nearer she got to Kingswell, the smaller and more closely packed the houses became until, in the town itself, it was almost impossible to find remnants of the once attractive little

market town. Progress, if it could be called that, had
reduced everything to a drab monotony of shape and
design that made one think of the houses children make
with their building blocks.

"And I suppose we're at least partly responsible because it was we who brought commerce to Kingswell
and built the very first works here—" Eleanor thought
as she had thought many times before. "But at least *our*
works aren't so hideously ugly as Stapleton's are—nor in
a place where you simply can't miss them, as theirs are!"

And, indeed, this was true. The Chalfont potteries
had been built when land was cheap, and their two and
sometimes only one-storied buildings which sprawled
over three times the area of ground that the Stapleton
works occupied were set in gardens that were Simon's
pride as they had been his father's and grandfather's.
Just now, roses were in bud and within a few weeks
would burst into glorious and triumphant colour.
Stapleton's, on the other hand, could boast of nothing
more than an asphalt yard and car park.

As Eleanor drove through the wide open gates the
man on duty lifted his hand in salute, but Eleanor saw
there was a surprised expression on his face. He was, of
course, wondering why Uncle Simon wasn't sitting beside her as usual. And so, truth to tell, was Eleanor.
What could this telephone call be that made it necessary
for it to be kept so private? Not for a minute did she
really believe that it could have anything to do with
any sort of merger between Chalfont's and Stapleton's,
and yet it was strange that at the same time that the
rumour was undoubtedly going about, Uncle Simon
should have developed this most unusual secretiveness.

However, once she was in her office, which opened
off her uncle's bigger one, she had too much to do for
there to be any time for idle speculation.

She passed on the messages with which Simon had
entrusted her, typed the letters he had dictated, and
then began to type a long report he had given her yesterday—an unusual report for this time of year since it
was an exact and up-to-date statement of the firm's
financial position. Much more the sort of thing she was
used to preparing at the end of the year.

She was half way through it when her house-telephone bell rang.

"Oh, this is reception, Miss Chalfont," a girl's voice announced. "Can Mr. Chalfont see Mr. Jervis Stapleton, please?"

Involuntarily Eleanor gave a little gasp. Jervis Stapleton—the second generation of the family and generally reported to have more say in the conduct of the firm than his father now had—what on earth had he come to see Uncle Simon about? Why, never, since she had been here had such a thing happened—

"I'm sorry, but Mr. Chalfont isn't in yet, Muriel," she collected her wits sufficiently to say. "No," in answer to the obvious question, "I'm very sorry, but I don't know when he'll be in. He was waiting for a telephone call at home. Will you tell Mr. Stapleton that?"

A pause, and then:

"Mr. Stapleton says he'd be glad if you could spare him a minute, Miss Chalfont," the girl said with a note of apologetic doubt in her voice.

"Oh—" Eleanor glanced down at her watch and saw that it was already eleven o'clock. Surely Uncle Simon hadn't expected to be as late as all this? "Yes, very well, Muriel. Have him shown up."

Involuntarily she glanced at herself in the mirror above her mantelpiece, and seeing that she naturally wanted to look her best when meeting someone she instinctively called "the enemy" was relieved to see that her hair was immaculately smooth and her make-up perfect. That gave her confidence for what she instinctively felt was going to be a difficult interview. It helped, too, to remember what Geoff had said about "the crisp little outfit" she was wearing.

She went through to her uncle's room and almost immediately the door was opened and one of the uniformed messenger girls announced:

"Mr. Stapleton, Miss Chalfont."

Eleanor knew Jervis Stapleton slightly because they had occasionally met socially, though there had never been any business contact, and some of her confidence seeped away as he approached her. She had not realised before what a big, commanding figure he was. Or that the lines of his face were so harsh and his dark eyes so penetrating.

"Good morning, Miss Chalfont," he said briskly, holding out his hand. "I'm very much obliged to you for seeing me."

"Not at all," Eleanor replied all the more formally because she resented being compelled to take his hand. "Although I'm afraid I can't tell you any more than I've already passed on to you through the receptionist. My uncle has been delayed because he's waiting at home for a telephone call. I'm sorry you've had a fruitless trip, but it would have been better had you made an appointment—"

"Oh, but I did, Miss Chalfont," Jervis said coolly. "Naturally! One doesn't risk wasting time by not taking such a simple precaution."

Without answering him, Eleanor turned to her uncle's desk and picked up his desk diary.

"There's no mention here of any appointment, Mr. Stapleton," she told him frigidly. "You can see for yourself."

"Oh no, there wouldn't be," he said, ignoring the proffered diary. "We only made the appointment an hour ago over the phone."

"Over the telephone?" Eleanor repeated sharply. "Do you mean—" she bit her lip, vexed that she had said so much—and incidentally told him that she was not entirely in her uncle's confidence.

"That it was my call for which he was waiting? Yes, it was. And that's why I asked to see you, Miss Chalfont, rather than say what's in my mind for the receptionist to pass on to you."

There was a note of gravity in the way he spoke which Eleanor felt was a warning.

"I'm afraid I don't understand." She forced herself to speak steadily, but her heart missed a beat. "Please explain."

"I will," he promised—but he hesitated momentarily and she was almost sure he squared his shoulders before going on to say: "Your uncle and I discussed a matter of common interest to us both. It transpired that he wanted some information from me which meant I needed to look up various references. I said I could bring the information to him here at eleven. And to that he replied that the arrangement would suit him admirably and that—" his voice seemed to drag over the words. "I could rely on him being here as he intended leaving home immediately we rang off."

Eleanor's eyes widened as he glanced at his watch.

"How long does it take to get here from Kingsworthy House?" he asked. "Twenty—perhaps twenty-five minutes?"

"About that," Eleanor agreed, dry-lipped.

"In that case, since it was a quarter to ten when we finished speaking, he ought to have been here by—say, twenty-five past ten at a conservative estimate."

"He must have been unexpectedly delayed," Eleanor said quickly, but with very little conviction.

Jervis shook his head.

"In that case, he would surely have rung through either to me or to you giving some explanation," he asserted. "He's a singularly punctilious man in such matters, as you must surely know, Miss Chalfont."

She did know. Punctuality was something of an obsession with Uncle Simon. He regarded keeping anyone waiting in circumstances such as this to be not only unbusinesslike, but also the worst of manners.

"What—what are you suggesting, Mr. Stapleton?" she asked half apprehensively, half resentfully. "An accident?"

"That is a possibility, of course," he replied. "But what I had in mind was that—it seemed to me as if, during our conversation, Mr. Chalfont sounded extremely weary. He appeared to have to make a great effort to concentrate—" he gave her an enquiring look.

Uncle Simon *had* seemed tired, Eleanor remembered, particularly when Aunt Alice had rung through to him. But she was not going to say so to this man! She didn't know just what lay behind all this probing, but every instinct warned her that here was a man who would always put his own interests first—and she had no intention of helping him do that.

"I really can't say I've noticed anything," she told

Jervis coolly. "I think perhaps you've let your imagination—"

The sentence was never finished because the telephone in Eleanor's room rang, and with a terrible sense of impending disaster, she ran to answer it. After a moment's hesitation, Jervis followed her.

"Yes," she said breathlessly. "Eleanor speaking." And then, as her caller spoke, Jervis saw the colour drain from her face. "Yes—yes, of course. I'll come at once."

She rang off and turned to find herself face to face with her visitor. There was a question in those dark eyes—

"Uncle Simon has had a stroke," she blurted out. "They're afraid—"

Blindly she groped for support—and found it in the arms of the man she so mistrusted.

CHAPTER II

FOR a brief moment Eleanor surrendered to the comforting strength of Jervis's arms. Then, as she tried to free herself, she realised with an instinctive sense of panic just how strong he was. For, disregarding her obvious intention, he steered her to her chair, forced her to sit down and then, standing in front of her, hands on hips, demanded if there was any brandy available.

"I don't want any," Eleanor insisted quickly. "Particularly as I'm driving—" and tried to stand up, only to be pushed unceremoniously down again.

"Stay where you are," Jervis ordered curtly. "You're not going to drive. I am. And don't waste time arguing. *Is* there any brandy?"

"In that cupboard," Eleanor heard herself saying meekly, pointing to the wall cupboard.

Coolly Jervis poured out a fairly stiff shot, added water from the carafe on a side table and handed the glass to her.

"Take a sip of that, and then give me your car keys."

"But you don't know my car—" Eleanor protested, none the less handing over her keys.

His lips twisted slightly as if the remark amused him. "You're too modest, Miss Chalfont," he told her drily. "You—and your car—are very well known in Kingswell. At present, it's parked third from the right in the V.I.P. park. Now then, drink every drop of that brandy and meet me at the main entrance in three minutes. Got that?"

"Yes," Eleanor said rather breathlessly, and with a curt nod, he strode out of the room.

Hastily Eleanor did as she'd been told, grimacing over the strength of the drink Jervis had poured out, yet never considering the possibility of disobeying his orders. She picked up her handbag and was in the lift before she remembered that she must let someone know what had happened. She paused at the receptionist's desk.

"Oh, Muriel, I've had some bad news from home—" she began, but the girl interrupted her.

"I know, Miss Chalfont. Mr. Stapleton told me," she said, genuinely sympathetic, yet obviously a little bit excited at being involved, however slightly, in the drama of the moment. "He said not to tell anyone until you'd left, so that you wouldn't be delayed by anyone asking questions, but then to let Mr. Baird and Mr. Turnbull know. Is that right?"

"Yes, quite right." Eleanor, once again, felt rather breathless.

It was really as if Jervis had read her mind, for that was exactly what she had intended asking Muriel to do. The alternative explanation—that Jervis knew so much about the running of Chalfont's that he was perfectly safe in assuming those were the two men who should be told what had happened—did not occur to her.

She passed through the main swing doors at the exact moment that Jervis pulled up in her little car. He leant over, opened the door for her and a moment later their journey had begun—in complete silence. He didn't even ask, she thought resentfully, whether she had carried out his orders. He just took it for granted that she would.

Despite her anxiety for Uncle Simon she appreciated in a subconscious way that Jervis was a good driver. He gave all his attention to the job, and he drove quickly and confidently. But he took no unreasonable risks. Indeed, on one occasion she felt that he was being unnecessarily cautious, and involuntarily her hands lifted in protest. Instantly Jervis took his left hand off the wheel and laid it over hers. It was a reassuring gesture, but his accompanying comment held a criticism which made it clear that even the present circumstances didn't, in his eyes, excuse her impatience.

"Even though this is your car, Miss Chalfont, you, as passenger, don't give instructions. At least, not when I'm at the wheel! Please remember that!"

At any other time she would have told him exactly what she thought of his rudeness, but this wasn't the time to put him in his place, and in any case, they were going through the wide open gates of Kingsworthy House now. In a moment or two—

"Where do you want me to stop?" Jervis asked as they came in sight of the house.

"At the West Pavilion, please, Mr. Stapleton."

He nodded and a moment or two later pulled up outside the Pavilion. So quickly that it was clear she must have been watching at the window, Eleanor's mother rushed out.

"Oh, darling, isn't it absolutely ghastly—" she began impetuously, and then, seeing Jervis for the first time, she stopped short and looked a quick question at Eleanor.

"This is Mr. Stapleton, Mother," Eleanor said automatically. "He has very kindly driven me home—"

"Oh!" Kitty's mouth was almost as round as her eyes as she took this in. "Do you mean—one of *the* Stapletons?"

"I expect I come under that heading," Jervis said good-naturedly. "But I'm sure Miss Chalfont is anxious to know how her uncle is?"

"Yes—please, Mother?" Eleanor begged, and Kitty pouted very slightly.

"Well, really, I don't know," she said in an offended way. "Dr. Brierly is still with him, but since Edgar rang through in really the most abrupt way to say what had happened, he hasn't condescended to tell me anything—though I'm sure he's keeping Alice up to date."

Eleanor did not reply, but Jervis saw her wince slightly and deliberately called attention to himself.

"Please tell me, Miss Chalfont, if there's any way in which I can be of further assistance," he said crisply. "Because, if not, I'll be going—?"

"I really don't think there is anything." Eleanor did her best not to give any indication of the relief that his departure would bring in either her manner or her tone. "But thank you very much for offering—and for bringing me home. It helped a lot. Oh—but how are you going to get back to Kingswell? Will you take my car?"

"Thanks, no, there's no need for that. I'll pick up a bus at your gates. Goodbye!" And lifting his hand in an informal gesture of farewell, he strode off along the gravel drive.

"Well, really, what an extremely abrupt young man!" Mrs. Chalfont said indignantly.

"S'sh, Mother, he'll hear you," Eleanor warned, but her mother shrugged her shoulders.

"I don't care if he does," she declared. "No wonder there's always been such feeling against the Stapletons if that's a specimen of their behaviour! How on earth did he come to drive you home, Eleanor?" she added curiously.

It was the question which Eleanor had dreaded, for it was one which she couldn't answer without involving Uncle Simon and his affairs.

"He came to the office on business, and happened to be there when Uncle Edgar telephoned to me," she explained, and saw with a sinking heart that her mother was quick to put what really did now seem to be a reasonable interpretation on to Jervis's visit.

"Then there simply must be something in this talk about a merger," Mrs. Chalfont declared triumphantly. And then, seeing the way Eleanor's lips were pressed together, added defensively, "Well, I know, darling, it isn't perhaps the time to talk about it, but after all, what happens to Chalfont's does affect us all, and now that this has happened to Simon—"

"I know," Eleanor said quickly. "But don't let's talk about it now, Mother. It really doesn't seem quite—" she paused, listening intently. "Isn't that the telephone ringing?"

And without waiting for her mother's reply, she dashed into the Pavilion and found that it was the house phone bell that was ringing. She snatched it from its cradle.

"Yes?" she asked breathlessly.

"Miss Eleanor? Manning speaking. Mr. Edgar would be glad if you'd come up immediately, miss. As quick as you can, please, and—" there was a brief pause—"Mr. Edgar says *only* you, miss. On no account is anyone else to come."

"I'll come at once," Eleanor promised, and rang off. She turned to find her mother at her elbow. "Uncle Edgar wants me—quickly," she explained. "I think perhaps Uncle Simon—"

"Well, really—" there was hostility in Mrs. Chalfont's voice. "I don't think a young girl like you should be asked—"

But Eleanor was already out of the room. She ran along the colonnade and so into the big house. She had the key to the private door in her handbag, but before she could use it the door was opened by Manning, grave-faced and anxious.

"I saw you coming, Miss Eleanor," he explained in a subdued voice. "This way, please."

He led the way to Simon Chalfont's bedroom and stood aside for Eleanor to pass.

The room was dimly lit, for the curtains had been drawn against the flaunting May sunshine, but as she tiptoed across to the bed Eleanor's eyes became adjusted to the lack of light. She saw that Aunt Helen was sitting beside her brother, his hand in hers. Uncle Edgar was standing beside Dr. Brierly at the foot of the bed.

Dr. Brierly, an old family friend, came to Eleanor and took her hands in his.

"I'm glad you're here, Eleanor," he said softly so that no one else could hear. "Simon's got something on his mind. Something to do with you. I want you to do all you can to reassure him even if you can't make out what it's all about. And I don't think you will be able to. He's—bad. No good trying to pretend anything else. How he's still alive—well, go along, child. Do your best."

As Eleanor approached the bed, Helen Chalfont stood up and made way for her. Instinctively Eleanor took Simon's hand in hers and pressed it gently. He turned his head slowly as if he realised that she was there and his lips seemed to try to shape her name.

She waited silently, realising that he was trying desperately to find the strength to say what was in his mind. How different he looked from when she had seen him—why, only a few hours ago! Then he had certainly been tired, but he had been in full possession of all his faculties. Now—her heart ached pitifully—he was near the point of complete exhaustion, and there was an unmistakable shadow over his face.

She saw rather than heard that he was trying to speak and bent lower.

"I couldn't see what else to do," said the thin, breathless voice. "But—but it's going to be hard on you, Eleanor."

"Don't worry, Uncle," Eleanor said earnestly, though her heart failed her a little at the implied threat in his words. "I'm—pretty strong, you know."

His lips puckered in the faintest of smiles.

"You'll need to be," he whispered. His hand tightened with sudden surprising strength on hers. "And maybe you won't be able to forgive me, but—do your best, child. Promise me that!"

"I promise," Eleanor said steadily.

He sighed as if with satisfaction and his grasp of her hand slackened. There was no doubt about it, he was smiling now—as if, perhaps, he was thankful that he need make no further effort.

And Eleanor, assured by Dr. Brierly that she had done all and more than he had hoped to set Simon's mind at ease, went slowly out of the room wondering with increasingly apprehension just what it was she had promised.

*   *   *

A few days later she knew. Simon Chalfont had died in his sleep a few hours after Eleanor had seen him. And now, when he had been laid to rest in the old churchyard just across the road from the gates of Kingsworthy House, all his relatives were sitting round the big table of Simon's dining room, preparing to listen while Mr. Franklin, Simon's solicitor, told them what he had done with his money.

Sitting at the foot of the table, Eleanor was conscious of a feeling of revulsion. She had been genuinely fond of her uncle and now it seemed to her sensitive mind as if they were gathered round like vultures, each determined to get a good share of the spoil.

If only Geoff could have been there to give her courage! But no one had suggested that he should come, and though he was practically one of the family, or would be when they were married, she had not liked to make the suggestion herself. But that might be because of what Geoff himself had said.

"Well, I don't envy you," he had remarked when Eleanor had told him of Mr. Franklin's plan. "For one thing, it sounds too absurdly melodramatic for words, these days! The family solicitor reading the will after the funeral! I ask you! And then there are bound to be rows. Always are when anybody's got more than tuppence-ha'penny to leave—probably then as well. At least one person is bound to think they've not been treated fairly. I could name one absolute cert if she gets less than the lot—your dear aunt Alice, Mrs. Edgar Chalfont! If ever there was a predatory female, she's one! Thank goodness I don't come in on this!"

And now, as she looked at Aunt Alice, tense and wearing deeper mourning than anyone else, it was impossible not to feel that both she and Geoff had been right. There was something of the predatory bird about Alice Chalfont. The thin, beaky nose, the harsh aggressive voice, the bony hands that even in repose curled like talons—again Eleanor asked herself how *could* a kindly, gentle soul like Uncle Edgar have married such a woman? Uncle Simon's suggestion that it was due to the attraction of opposites didn't satisfy her. It was too slick, too easy.

Her eyes moved to Edgar Chalfont. So very like Simon in feature and colouring, and yet there was an unmistakable difference. Both men had grown beards, but whereas, seeing Simon, one would hardly have bothered even to say "Here's a man who chooses to wear a beard," in Edgar's case it was impossible not to wonder if its purpose was not to hide a weak chin—because Edgar *was* weak. To him it was such torment to live in an atmosphere of strife and argument that he was willing—anxious, even—to avoid it even at the cost of surrendering his own self-respect.

Suddenly Mr. Franklin cleared his throat and every head turned towards him. In his hands he held what was obviously Simon Chalfont's will, but he seemed to be reluctant to start reading it, for instead he made a discursive and rather pointless statement about the present conditions of the stock market and the consequent difficulty in assessing just what Simon's investments were worth.

Eleanor felt herself growing more and more tense, and so did everyone else, judging by the nervy little movements of more than one person's hands, and the way in which they indulged in meaningless little coughs. It wasn't difficult to imagine that the same thought was in each mind—why doesn't he tell us what Simon's done with his money? Is it because he knows it's going to cause trouble?

And then at last, rather hurriedly, Mr. Franklin began to read. The will began with bequests of certain personal possessions. Their mother's jewellery to his sister Helen. His own jewellery to his brother Edgar and so on. Various provisions for employees who, like Manning, had been with him for a long time. Details of a trust which would provide Kitty with a life income equal to the allowance he had made her. A similar provision for Alice if her husband predeceased her.

Alice's sniff on hearing this was a triumph in its way, for it expressed all the dislike she had always felt for a woman so much more attractive than herself, and in addition, her conviction that Kitty had used her good looks to get round their brother-in-law to make her reasonably independent while Alice herself got nothing unless Edgar died.

But, like everyone else present, she felt that so far nothing of real importance had been announced. No one knew just what Simon had to leave, but everyone knew that he was a wealthy man, and so far, it could only be a fraction of his wealth with which Mr. Franklin had dealt.

Then, deliberately, almost defiantly, Mr. Franklin read out a clause that for all its clarity was so astonishing that for a moment no one seemed capable of taking it in.

Then Alice jumped to her feet, her face twitching with passion.

"Do you—do you mean to say he's left everything else—his share in the firm, this house—all the rest of his money to—*Eleanor*?" she demanded shrilly.

"Yes," Mr. Franklin told her suavely. "Just that!"

"But it's absurd—outrageous!" Alice declared, a rising note of hysteria in her voice. "Simon must have been out of his mind—we shall contest this—"

"No, Alice." Edgar spoke very quietly. He stared down at his hands, loosely linked on the table before him, as if he could not bring himself to look at his wife. "We shall do nothing of the sort. I have been aware of what Simon intended doing since he first made up his mind about it—and I agreed with him that, in the circumstances, it was the wisest course—"

"You agreed with him—" Alice's voice had sunk to a harsh whisper. "You *agreed* with him!" She laughed scornfully. "Yes, you would! You've always let Simon rule you—and look where it's got you! So few shares in the firm that you might as well have none for all the good they do you and for the rest, Simon's employee—that's what you've been! And now I suppose you'll be perfectly content to take your orders from Eleanor—"

Edgar stood up.

"That will do, Alice," he said with an authority that no one had ever heard from him before. "You've already said far too much, and for that, I apologise on your behalf. Now, you will come home with me—at once!"

And to the surprise and relief of the remainder of the

family, Alice did as she was told without another word.

Edgar opened the door for her and then paused.

"I'll be glad, Eleanor, if a little later, we could have a talk together?"

"Yes, of course, Uncle Edgar," Eleanor said through dry lips.

He went out and closed the door behind them. There was a moment's silence. Then Helen said thoughtfully :

"Of course, I can appreciate why Simon's done this. You have worked with him and know more about the running of the firm than anyone else in the family can possibly do, including Edgar. He's never been a business man and it's far too late for him to start now. It's the practical and the art side of the work that interests him. Yes, I can see how Simon's mind worked. But it's hard on you, child!" She stood up and laid her hand gently on Eleanor's shoulder. "I want you to know one thing, my dear. Unlike Edgar, I had no previous knowledge of Simon's intentions, but I accept what he has done and I will do nothing to increase the problems that are ahead of you! Drop in and see me soon—though not for the next week. I've struck a snag in my present book and I'm going to be late finishing it if I'm not careful. Goodbye, Kitty—Mr. Franklin."

She went out of the room, a trim, petite figure who had carved her own niche in life and who, Eleanor realised gratefully, envied no one. Kitty saw her from a different viewpoint.

"What an extraordinary person she is!" she exclaimed, evidently forgetting that Mr. Franklin was still there. "It must come of writing all those whodunits ! Fancy pitying you, Eleanor ! Why, you must be a frightfully wealthy woman, isn't she, Mr. Franklin?"

"She is," Mr. Franklin agreed drily. "But wealth brings its own responsibility and problems, just as poverty does, you know, Mrs. Chalfont."

"Well, I know which sort I'd sooner have !" Kitty declared gaily. "But there's something in what you say. You're going to have trouble with Alice, Eleanor, whatever Edgar may say. She's the dangerous sort that isn't so much ambitious for herself as for her children, and I wouldn't be surprised if she hadn't made up her mind that Edgar was going to be the chief beneficiary—which would have meant *her*, really! Yes, I'm beginning to see what Helen meant! Never mind, darling. I'll keep her at bay for you, and if you feel like adding a little something to what really isn't a very large allowance in the circumstances—well, I shan't say no!" And her blue eyes sparkled with anticipatory enjoyment.

Eleanor did not reply. What was there to say? Perhaps in time her mother, as well as Aunt Alice, would understand that Uncle Simon had left her more than money. He had left her a trust to run not only the potteries but also the family affairs to the best advantage of everyone concerned. And that meant—no favourites. No wonder he had said it was going to be hard on her and had asked for her forgiveness!

Mr. Franklin's dry voice cut across her thoughts.

"I have a letter here for you, Miss Chalfont," he said, handing it to her. "On the day that your uncle collapsed, Manning found this on his desk and very properly gave it to me. I've no idea of its contents, so perhaps you will let me know later if it is in any way concerned with the settlement of the estate?"

Eleanor promised and Mr. Franklin took his departure. Kitty gave a little sigh.

"Well, that's all over, thank goodness!" she said cheerfully. "Now life can get started again!" She strolled round the room, examining the beautiful old mahogany furniture with a critical eye. "You know, Eleanor, valuable though this is, I do find it rather depressingly heavy. I think it would be a good idea if we got rid of it and refurnished entirely when we move over here."

"When we move over here?" Eleanor was too startled at the suggestion to be able to hide her astonishment. "But we're not going to do that, Mother. We're perfectly comfortable where we are."

"Are we?" Kitty sniffed disparagingly. "In that poky little rabbit hutch? Why, it's absurd to think of remaining there when we might be here! Particularly, as you must remember, now that you're head of the house. You've got to keep up appearances, Eleanor. It will be expected of you. Your place is here!"

"Oh, heavens," Eleanor thought desperately. "Is everyone going to make it as difficult as possible for me? Doesn't anybody understand that I'm honour bound to Uncle Simon to make any decisions myself, not let other people make them for me?"

With all her heart she wished that she could run away and hide—shirk all the responsibilities that had been thrust so ruthlessly on her. But of course, that wasn't possible—

"So that's settled," Kitty went on complacently. "And don't worry that it will be any bother to you, darling. I'll see to everything."

It had to be done here and now, however distasteful it might be. Eleanor squared her shoulders.

"I'm sorry, Mother," she said gently but with unmistakable firmness, "but I can't agree to your plans. I've no intention of getting rid of this lovely furniture. Why, it's part of the house! And as for you and me living here—aren't you forgetting that I shall be marrying Geoff in a few months' time? And while I can't say that he and I will be living here then until I've discussed it with him, it's an obvious possibility—so it would be rather silly to make what could only be a temporary arrangement."

She saw the dismay in her mother's pretty face—dismay and something else. The hurt look of a little girl who has been smacked for doing something she hadn't realised was naughty. And suddenly Eleanor felt herself to be years older—much older than her mother—

"Oh," Kitty said disconsolately. "I'd forgotten about Geoff!"

And she trailed out of the room looking so dejected that Eleanor was on the point of calling her back—of easing her sense of guilt by compromising in some way. Then her eyes fell on Uncle Simon's letter, and she knew she must read that before she made any plans at all.

*   *   *

The letter was a long one, and Eleanor read it twice before she felt she had mastered the full significance of its contents.

The date on which Simon Chalfont had written it was the day on which he had died, and it began:

My dear Eleanor,

I've been doing a lot of thinking lately because I'm reasonably sure I've had notice to quit. Not, perhaps, in the very near future, but I've been warned, both by Dr. Brierly, and by my own inner conviction. And I'm of the opinion that one can't be mistaken when the real thing is near.

Well, there it is, my dear. It could happen any day —today, tomorrow, months (but I don't think years) ahead. For the sake of everyone concerned, and you in particular, I've got to assume that it may be before I've had time to make up my mind on a very important matter which, even if it were to prove to be an astute business move, would almost certainly bring changes which might well prove to be unacceptable to the people for whom I care most—my family.

You will not be given this letter until after my death, and then only if I have not made a decision— something that cannot be delayed long.

The telephone call about which I made something of a mystery—and for which I am still waiting, by the way—will come from young Jervis Stapleton. That surprises you, doesn't it? Our detested rivals! What follows may even shock you. What is under discussion is nothing less than a merger between Chalfont's and Stapleton's—

Eleanor caught her breath. So the gossip that both her mother and Geoff had heard had been the truth after all! It was, indeed, a shock, as Uncle Simon had predicted. She turned back to his letter.

It was Stapleton's who made the first approach. They—particularly young Jervis—are of the opinion that one way and another, we and they are cutting each other's throats in the markets, and, moreover, that if we were to combine and make one firm, we could enter into competition with other large firms with every hope of success.

My first reaction was to turn the suggestion down

flat. I was, in fact, half vexed, half amused by it. But the longer I hesitated—and naturally, one can't just dismiss a thing like that off-hand—the less sure I felt.

There is a lot in the idea. And we and they have this in common—each firm honestly gives the best value possible at the price charged. Yes, that's true, Eleanor, though I admit prejudice has made me reluctant to admit it.

Our finished article is first class, and consequently costly because our processes are expensive. Stapleton's, on the other hand, produce an excellent second class standard which they can and do sell more cheaply. Sometimes we miss a market because we are too costly, sometimes they do because their work isn't quite fine enough. If, in these cases, the clients simply dropped Chalfont's and went to Stapleton's, or *vice versa*, we would neither of us lose in the long run. But is that what happens? Sometimes. Not always. And that is the undoubted fact on which Stapleton's base their suggestion. Combined, we could offer clients a much wider range than either of us can do now, and both firms would gain thereby.

So why haven't I already agreed? I'll tell you. Because I'm old, Eleanor. Because I don't like change. Because I just want life to go jogging quietly on as it has done for years.

And yet—and yet—there is another side to it. Bringing such a merger into existence would undoubtedly be a very tiring and troublesome business. But once it was over—

You don't, I think, know much about young Jervis. He is undoubtedly a live wire—and a hard worker, which isn't always the same thing. His father is gradually handing over the reins to him, and clearly has every confidence in the boy. From what I've seen of him, I think he is more than likely justified.

Now I know, you know, and he, dear fellow, is the first to admit, that Edgar has not a head for business. That he's always left to me, and it's worked out very well. I've always tried to make decisions which are to his benefit as well as my own, and he, despite any difficulties, has given me unswerving loyalty. Of course he knows about this idea—since he is a partner, this is naturally the case, but he wants to leave the decision to me.

And there, Eleanor, he is wrong. Because, I honestly believe for the first time in my business life, I know I'm being swayed by personal feeling. Do you see what I mean?

If I say "no" will it be because I can't face the effort it will require to put the deal through.

If I say "yes" will it be because I welcome the knowledge that I, like Jervis's father, could let his young shoulders bear what has hitherto been my burden.

You see my difficulty? It is a very genuine one. In my heart I want to do the right thing—but I can't judge dispassionately, as I know I ought to. So far I've hedged and prevaricated. Even today, I know I'm going to ask for some more figures to study—anything to put off making the decision. But it can't go on.

Perhaps I can't, either. Perhaps that's the solution. I've a feeling it might be. And that's why I'm writing to you now.

You, if you read this letter, will have to be the one to make the decision. And it must be *your* decision. No one else's, my dear, either living or dead. All that I ask is that you will face up to all the implications, weigh them, and then, without bias or prejudice, make your decision.

And by now, Eleanor, you may be feeling that I owe you an apology for putting such a burden on you. Yet who else is there? You know most about the firm, you've a good business head, and, I firmly believe, both integrity and courage. You'll need that.

And that, I think, is all I have to say. No, there is one thing more. I told you, just a short time ago, that when you get married, you will no longer be able to work for me because I believe it would be unfair to your husband. If that is so, and I believe it is, when you will be taking the comparatively limited responsibility of being my secretary, how much more so is it if you are the senior partner of the firm? No, child, I'm not asking you to give up any idea of marriage.

But I am asking you to consider seriously the wisdom of deferring your marriage for a year—a year that you will find difficult whether you go ahead with this merger or not.

Think it over, Eleanor. And try not to bear me any malice for what I've done.

Ah, the telephone bell is ringing! I'm afraid that young man will be vexed at being fobbed off once again! He likes his own way—but then, so do I! Even the telephone bell sounds impatient.

Good luck, my dear,
Your loving uncle
SIMON CHALFONT.

Eleanor put the letter down with hands whose trembling she could not control.

For the moment one thing and one thing only that her uncle had written filled her mind.

The year ahead would be difficult whether or not she went ahead with the merger. So difficult that her private life would have to take second place. So difficult that it would be unfair to both Geoff and herself to submit their early married life to such stresses and strains.

But what would Geoff say to the idea of postponing their marriage?

And what did her own heart say?

CHAPTER III

FOR a while Eleanor sat very still. She could think of nothing but her personal and surely almost unsolvable problems. Then gradually came the realisation that, despite what Uncle Simon had said about the necessity of any decision being hers alone, she must first find out what other people concerned thought about the situation. How else could she, as Uncle Simon had wished, face up to the implications and weigh them up?

And obviously, the first person whose opinion she must seek was her uncle Edgar's—as he, apparently, had already appreciated.

She rang through on the house phone to the East Pavilion, and to her relief, Edgar answered. She made her request, and a few minutes later he arrived. He looked very tired, Eleanor thought. Almost as tired as Uncle Simon had looked, and yet, rather strangely, there was a dignity in his bearing and even an air of self-assurance about him that she had never seen before.

"Thank you for acceding to my request so promptly, my dear," he said, sitting down on the opposite side of the desk from his brother's chair which Eleanor now occupied. "In my opinion, there are one or two matters which it is necessary for me to mention without delay. The first is Simon's will. As I've already said, I knew its terms, and though I felt he was putting a very heavy burden on your young shoulders if he did die in the near future, none the less, it was a personal relief to me." He sighed and shook his head. "I've no head for business, you know, Eleanor. Never had. I know that and so did Simon. A pity, perhaps, but there it is. I was always at the bottom of any form at school, with the only decent marks for things I did with my hands. I'm still like that, and it's too late for me to change, even if I wanted to, which I don't. You do understand that, don't you?" he finished anxiously.

"I think what you're trying to say is that I don't have to worry whether your feelings are being hurt if I make a decision," Eleanor said gently.

"That's it!" Edgar said with relief. "I'll give you the same loyalty I gave to Simon, Eleanor, but it's for you to make the decisions. And that brings me to the other thing—" He hesitated and gave her a dubious glance. "Did Simon tell you that we've been approached by Stapleton's with a suggestion that there should be a merger?"

"He didn't tell me before," Eleanor explained. "But he left me a letter telling all about it."

"Ah!" There was no mistaking the relief in Edgar's

sigh. "And he told you what he had decided to do?"

"No, he didn't. I wish he had! It would have made it easier to decide—but you'd better read the letter for yourself." And she pushed it across the desk towards him.

Edgar read it through and then laid it down. He sat in silence, and once again he was staring down at his loosely linked hands—a favourite trick of his in moments of perplexity or distress.

"Well?" Eleanor asked, trying not to sound too impatient. "What's your opinion, Uncle Edgar? For you must surely have one!"

"Yes, I have," he agreed heavily. "But I doubt if it's of much value because, like Simon's, it's the outcome of personal feelings, not of balanced reasoning. Not that my point of view is the same as his was. In my case, it's the outcome of sentiment and prejudice. Even though I've had little to do with the management of it, it's always been *our* firm to me. And I want it to remain that way. But if this merger goes through, it won't. It can't. An outsider will have at least part control, and that outsider would, of all people, be a Stapleton! That really does go against the grain. I've always felt that Stapletons were a second rate firm doing a second rate job, and unlike Simon, I've not changed my mind. What's more, I've always had the impression that they weren't too fastidious if they got the chance of putting over a smart bit of business. I wouldn't like Chalfont's to get tarred with that particular brush! And yet is all that really true? I've been asking myself where I got my prejudices from, and there's only one answer—from my father. He and old Stapleton—the founder of the firm—hated one another like poison, all the more because they'd been friends at one time. Father was convinced that Stapleton's would go broke in next to no time, but they didn't, and that made him more prejudiced than ever. And I took his word for it that the less we had to do with them, the better. But that's ancient history. It doesn't help much at the present moment. Maybe young Stapleton is perfectly honest in his belief that we'd both be better off as one firm. But I don't know, Eleanor. I just don't know!"

And more than that he would not say, except to point out that at her age, the future belonged far more to her than to him at his, and that since she'd have to abide by the results longer than he would, it was really only right that the decision should be hers—

*   *   *

Once again, when Edgar had gone, the house telephone bell rang. To Eleanor it was the last straw. Deliberately ignoring it, she made her escape through the back of the house, and so to the stable yard.

More than anything else in the world she wanted at that moment to get away from Kingsworthy House—away from the people who, for one reason or another, were forcing her to assume an authority that went against her every inclination.

"Because I'm *not* a career woman," she told herself passionately as she got her little car out of the coach-house-turned-garage. "I want to get married, and make a real home for Geoff and me, and have a family—and for that to be my entire world. Not be the boss and give orders as if I was a man. And though a man can run a job and enjoy home life, I don't think a woman can—"

And that, of course, was what was really troubling her. She knew that Uncle Simon had been right. It wasn't fair to Geoff or herself, or their marriage, for her to try to do both jobs—and yet how could she bear to postpone her wedding day?

She had assumed that Geoff would be out somewhere giving riding instruction, but he surprised her by leaning out of an open window of his flat above the stable buildings.

"Hallo, I thought it sounded like your car," he said cheerfully. "Where are you off to?"

"I'm runing away," Eleanor said succinctly.

"Good idea," Geoff approved, evidently not noticing that she had not returned his smile. "Hold on, and I'll run away with you!"

Her lips parted to tell him that perhaps it would be better if he didn't come—that she wasn't likely to be very good company just now—but before she could get the words out, he drew in his head and closed the window. A moment or so later she heard him clatter rapidly down the uncarpeted stairs.

He was smiling—that charming, infectious smile that always made Eleanor's heart turn over. It did now, and yet she found it quite impossible to respond to it. And as he came towards her, his own smile faded.

"Had about enough?" he asked sympathetically, and she nodded in silence.

"That confounded family of yours!" Geoff exploded wrathfully. "Of course, they would only see it from their own point of view instead of realising what an intolerable burden your uncle has put on you!"

Eleanor stared at him, considerably taken aback. "Who told you? Surely not Uncle Edgar or Aunt Alice?"

"Well, no." Geoff coloured slightly and ran his fingers through his fair hair as if to hide the embarrassment her very direct question had caused him to feel. "Young Celia told me, as a matter of fact. She overheard her parents—well, discussing it, shall we say!"

"And she listened?" Eleanor asked distastefully.

"Well, she could hardly help it," Geoff defended eighteen-year-old Celia quickly. "You know how your aunt's voice carries—particularly when she's angry about something. And she certainly is over this! And quite frankly, I'm not surprised! I always thought your uncle Simon was a thoroughly practical, businesslike man, but this is simply crazy!"

Already Eleanor had realised what a gulf the new situation had created between her and the rest of the family, but until this moment she had not realised just how complete her isolation was.

"So you're going to side with them against me?" she said, hardly above a whisper.

"I'm doing nothing of the sort," Geoff denied indignantly. "I'm simply clear-sighted enough to appreciate what you'll be up against—and the pity of it is that your Uncle Simon didn't see it as well! Oh, I know, these days women take on jobs that were always regarded as only suitable for men, but if you ask me, they probably find it a lot harder to make out simply because of their sex! Look how many times you hear women saying they'd rather work for a man than for another woman. And do you honestly think that a man really likes taking orders from a woman? Because I jolly well know they don't! I wouldn't myself."

"No, I know, there is a lot of prejudice," Eleanor said wearily. "But I think without doubt Uncle Simon did think of all that. And what else was there that he could do? Uncle Edgar—" She paused, but Geoff had no difficulty in knowing what was in her mind.

"No, that would never have done," he said, grimacing expressively. "The way things are in that household, to do that would have been exactly the same as handing everything over to your Aunt Alice. And that would have been disastrous. At the very least, you'd have had strikes on your hands, and you'd probably end by going bankrupt into the bargain."

"Well then?" Eleanor asked. "Who does it leave? Celia and Richard? At eighteen they're both too young and too inexperienced to take on a job like this. That only leaves Aunt Helen. Admittedly she's brilliantly clever—but in her own particular line. She knows nothing about running a business nor about the actual processes we use, and I very much doubt if she'd be interested in finding out. In any case, why should she? She loves the work she's doing and she's earning a very good income doing it. She'd be crazy to make a change at her age."

"Yes," Geoff admitted grudgingly, "I suppose so."

"So whom does that leave?" Eleanor asked significantly.

There was, she knew, only one answer to that, but with an uneasy movement of his shoulders, Geoff showed how reluctant he was to accept it.

"Oh, I grant you, it's all very difficult, but there must be some way out for you. I wish to goodness there had been something in that rumour about Chalfont's linking up with Stapleton's! That would have been an easy way out."

Eleanor's eyes fell from his and she didn't reply. So far as she knew, no one but herself and Uncle Edgar knew the truth about the merger, and it seemed unlikely that he had passed on the information to Aunt Alice, because if he had, it would surely have been mentioned so that Celia would have heard all about it and would have told Geoff. And very clearly, that was not the case.

Eleanor was not at all sure that she should, or wanted to discuss it with anyone, even Geoff, before she had made up her mind what to do. But as the silence between them lengthened, Geoff put his own interpretation to it.

"There is something in it, isn't there, Eleanor?" he said urgently.

"Yes," she said unwillingly. "But—"

Geoff opened the car door on the driver's side.

"Move over," he said crisply, and as, automatically, she did as he requested, he slid into the driver's seat and pressed the self-starter.

"Geoff, what are you going to do?" Eleanor demanded anxiously. And then, as he slid expertly out of the yard and down the drive: "Geoff, where are we going?"

"Somewhere quiet where there's no chance of interruptions," he told her grimly. "We're going to thrash this business out without any waste of time, because if we don't—" he left the sentence unfinished, but there was an ominous significance even in that.

He drove quickly and expertly for several miles away from direction of the town until, taking a side turning, he eventually came out on the top of a fairly steep hill, the view from which was famous.

But at that moment, the view did not interest Geoff.

"Now then," he said inexorably as he stopped the car and switched off the ignition, "there's no chance of us being overheard and we'll see in time if anybody is coming up the hill. So let's hear all about it, Eleanor!"

"I'm not sure if I can—" Eleanor replied uncertainly. "You see—"

"I see one thing very clearly," Geoff said bitterly. "Even in so short a time since you've known about this business, you've changed into a totally different person from the one you were!"

"That's not fair," Eleanor said indignantly. "I haven't changed in the least. It's just that I'm bewildered by all that's happened. Anyone would be in my shoes. *You* would be, Geoff!"

"Maybe," he admitted. "But if I *were* in your shoes, Eleanor, I know what I'd do—get out of them as quickly as possible!"

"But how can I?" Eleanor protested helplessly. "If, when he was alive, Uncle had asked me to take over managing Chalfont's, I've have told him I couldn't do it. But I haven't been asked. I haven't been given a choice. It's—it's been wished on me—and you can't argue with the dead, Geoff."

"You can refuse to accept a bequest," he insisted dogmatically. "And if you've got any sense, that's what you will do!"

"But how can I?" Eleanor found it difficult not to let a note of impatience creep into her voice. "If I were to do that, it would be the same as if Uncle Simon had died intestate—"

"So what?" Geoff, on the other hand, didn't try to hide his impatience. "In that case, what he left would be divided between his next of kin—your Uncle Edgar, your Aunt Helen and you, as your father's daughter. Or something like that."

"No," Eleanor said firmly. "That wouldn't do, because I know that it would be going absolutely against what Uncle Simon wanted. And I know *why* he didn't want it that way. So do you, Geoff."

"Perhaps I do," he agreed reluctantly. "And looking at it from his point of view, no doubt it's understandable enough. But there are other points of view, you know. Mine, for instance." He turned towards her, took her firmly by the shoulders and forced her to look at him. "Had you thought of that? Have you considered just what sort of a mess it would make of our early married life if you were tied hand and foot to those confounded works? And don't tell me that you'd be boss and could suit yourself what hours you worked, because that's nonsense. If *you* slack so would everybody else, and then where would you be?"

Eleanor swallowed convulsively, but she did not reply, and Geoff, his eyes narrowing, studied her face intently.

"You've got something on your mind, haven't you,

Eleanor?" he said slowly. "Something you haven't got the nerve to tell me. But you're going to, you know. So let's have it!"

And, as Eleanor could still not find the courage to tell him what Uncle Simon had asked of her, his face darkened.

"No? Then I'll have to work it out for myself, won't I? And I think I can. We'll start with an impression that I got from your uncle. I'm reasonably certain that, had he lived, he wouldn't have agreed to you continuing as his secretary because he didn't think a married woman would give him the undivided loyalty he demanded—right? Yes, I am, aren't I? I could feel you tense up when I said that! So now we'll look at the other side of the coin. By leaving everything to you, he's committed you to staying on at the office, hasn't he? So I think he has at least asked you to give up the idea of marriage—"

"No, Geoff, not that!" Eleanor told him just too eagerly. "He would have known I wouldn't agree to that—"

"Then what did he want you to do?" Geoff demanded. "Because there was something, I'll swear!"

"He—he wanted me to—to postpone getting married for a year," Eleanor stumbled over the words, seeing the cloud of anger that darkened his face. "But, honestly, it was as much for your sake as for anything else—"

Geoff laughed harshly.

"Spare me, my dear! That's a bit too much for me to swallow," he said ironically.

"But it's true, Geoff," Eleanor insisted earnestly. "It is, really. You see, you were right in saying that Uncle wouldn't have let me go on working for him once we were married—"

"Indeed?" Geoff raised his fair brows. "And you didn't think that worth mentioning to me, though, seeing we've calculated on having your income to begin with when we get married, it was certainly my business!"

"But he only told me on the morning of the day he died," Eleanor explained, her heart sinking as she saw that his face did not clear. She had so relied on Geoff standing by her, and now this interview was proving the most difficult of all! "And since then—"

"All right, since then the whole set-up has changed," Geoff finished. "So why mention that at all?"

"Because Uncle referred to it," Eleanor explained. "What he said, as near as I can remember, was that he had said that it wouldn't be fair to you, because of my divided loyalty to you and the firm. So even more, with me as senior partner to the firm, it would be unfair."

"So he suggested we shouldn't be married for a year," Geoff said thoughtfully.

"Yes. And after all, Geoff, since we weren't going to get married for three months in any case, that only means an extra nine months, doesn't it?" Eleanor pointed out eagerly.

"Does it?" he asked sceptically. "I'm not so sure, Eleanor! What makes you think that, having got yourself deeply involved in the management of the firm during that year that you'd be able to get out of it later?"

"Well—perhaps not get out of it, exactly," Eleanor admitted. "But during that time I would have learnt the ropes thoroughly which would mean it wouldn't take up so much of my time, and I'd surely have been able to find people to whom I could delegate some of the responsibility."

"Sounds quite plausible," Geoff admitted. "But I'm not convinced. Shall I tell you what I think, Eleanor? I think—I'm quite sure that if we once postpone our wedding, we'll never get married. And what's more," he went on doggedly, ignoring her cry of protest, "your Uncle Simon was banking on that!"

"But that's nonsense, Geoff," Eleanor protested vigorously. "Why should he feel like that?"

"Two reasons, my dear. One, that he hoped you'd get so interested in your job that at the end of the year you wouldn't *want* to have any other claim on your time and loyalty. And the other—hasn't it occurred to you how very different the situation is from what it was? I proposed to a girl who had little or no money of her own. But now, out of the blue, I'm suddenly engaged to an heiress! Or, to look at it from another point of view, and the one I believe your uncle saw it from, here are you, an heiress, lumbered with a man who's next door to a failure from a wealthy man's standpoint. Someone who will either be content to sponge on you or who, if he's got any pride—and I have, Eleanor —will get increasingly resentful at having to live up to a standard beyond what he himself could provide for his wife. It's an impossible situation—and the old man wanted to make sure that you had more than the next three months in which to find that out!"

"It—it almost sounds as if you're going to be the one that breaks it off, not me," Eleanor said tremulously.

"I'm not sure I wouldn't save both of us a lot of heart-burning if I did," Geoff said morosely. "Unless, of course, there is some way out—this business about the merger with Stapleton's, for example. We've somehow sidetracked from that. Just what are the terms of the merger? And who originated the idea?"

"Stapleton's made the suggestion," Eleanor explained. "But there isn't a merger yet. It was under discussion, but Uncle Simon couldn't make up his mind whether to agree or not."

"Oh?" Geoff said with interest. "Why not?"

As briefly and clearly as possible, Eleanor explained Simon Chalfont's predicament, and when she had finished, Geoff nodded.

"Yes, I see his point," he said thoughtfully, tapping with his fingers on the edge of the car door. "A lot of preliminary and concentrated fuss, which the old man didn't feel up to, but the other side of that, a considerable lessening of the burden. D'you know what, Eleanor, I wouldn't be surprised if it wasn't worrying about what decision he should make that brought on that last attack."

"I know. I've thought of that," Eleanor said in a low voice. "And it doesn't make me feel particularly inclined to do what the Stapletons—and I think it's principally the son, Jervis—wants."

"I don't think you ought to let personal feelings come into it," Geoff said rather surprisingly. "What you've got to do is to consider it dispassionately with a view to deciding just how good the terms are that you're likely

to get out of Stapleton's. That's really the deciding
factor, isn't it? Whether it's worth while or not financially."

"Yes, I suppose so," Eleanor agreed listlessly.

"But of course it is, my dear girl! I may not have
made much of a success of my own affairs but at least
I can see that!" He rubbed his hand thoughtfully over
his chin. "That request of your uncle's, Eleanor—was it
incorporated in his will? I mean, was it a condition of
you inheriting his fortune?"

"No, it wasn't. He wrote a letter to me that morning—" Eleanor explained. "But—"

"Oh, good!" Geoff smiled for the first time since
their conversation had begun. "That simplifies it considerably."

"Does it?" Eleanor said doubtfully. "But surely it's
morally just as binding—"

"That's a matter of opinion, and it isn't mine," Geoff
declared crisply. "The point is, it certainly isn't *legally*
binding. Now then—you say Stapleton's approached
your uncle—and they suggested a merger. And that's
something they certainly wouldn't have done if they
didn't see something to be gained by it. Right?"

"Well, yes, of course," Eleanor agreed.

"Then, my dear girl, don't you see, you've got the
whip hand! It's for you to dictate the terms—and what
I suggest is that you tell them you're not interested in a
merger, but you'd consider selling outright. At your
price, of course!"

"Oh!" Eleanor gasped, totally unprepared for such
a suggestion. "But suppose they said they wouldn't consider that?"

Geoff shrugged his shoulders.

"Something in that," he agreed. "No, I don't know
that there is. Look, you could make it clear that you
don't mind carrying on as your own boss, or getting
right out and leaving Stapleton's in possession—but a
merger would mean constant compromise—"

"I'm not sure that it would," Eleanor interrupted.
"Not from the little I've seen of Jervis Stapleton. I
think he'd take it for granted that he would be the one
to lay down the law and I'd just do what I was told,

regardless of what the terms of a merger might be."

"You don't like him?" Geoff asked, looking at her through narrowed eyes.

"Oh—" Eleanor's shoulders moved uneasily. "I suppose I ought not to say it because, actually, as I told you, he was with me when the news about Uncle Simon came through, and he was most helpful in a very practical way. But—" she hesitated, trying to find just the right words—"he made me feel that it wasn't out of kindness that he took charge, but because he took it for granted that I just wasn't competent to cope on my own."

"Yes, he does give the impression of being a bit over-sure of himself," Geoff agreed thoughtfully. "And that could make for difficulties in running as a combined firm. Actually, it's a situation that's almost impossible to assess because there's so much more to it than the drawing up of a legal document. There are personalities to be taken into account." He paused as if he was considering what he had just said. Then he went on deliberately, "Well, as I see it, there is a choice of three courses open to you—to merge, not to merge—or to sell out. But what you've got to remember is this, Eleanor. Not only is there nobody who has the right to tell you what you ought to do, but—and this is perhaps more important than you realise—*you* as well as everybody else concerned will have to stand by the decision you make, whatever its outcome may be."

And without waiting for her to reply, he switched on the ignition, set the car in motion and drove back to Kingsworthy House in a silence which Eleanor didn't have the ability—or perhaps the wish—to break.

*   *   *

For the next fortnight Eleanor was busier than she had ever been in her life before. Part of her time had to be spent at the office, of course, and there were innumerable interviews with senior staff as she set about the task of turning herself from being a secretary into being the controlling force. And it wasn't easy. More than once she felt she detected a resentment, however slight, from men who clearly weren't too pleased to know that in future they must take their orders from a woman.

Then, though she had to a great extent been in her uncle's confidence, she found that in some ways, perhaps wisely, he had kept his own counsel. For she found that he had kept diaries which recorded not only business events but also his very frank opinions about both things and people. Eleanor felt rather mean and under-handed in reading of the various delinquencies among the staff of which she had previously known nothing, but none the less, it was from the diaries that she gained a deeper knowledge of the firm's affairs than she could ever have done from any other source.

Among other incidents, Simon Chalfont had recorded all that had taken place between the two firms since Jervis Singleton had first broached the question of a merger some two months earlier.

With interest Eleanor read that Simon's first reaction had been one of complete rejection. It seemed sheer impertinence to him that a *nouveau riche* firm such as Stapleton's should make such a proposal to an old stand-ing one like Chalfont's. But two days later he was lunching with Jervis Singleton, and the entry following the luncheon made it clear that at least he had been persuaded to see that there were two sides to the question. Later came the admission that there might be something in it. Then an ominous entry—

"My heart played me up today—the first time in six months. Not a severe attack, but no doubt Brierly would call it a warning. I suppose it means I'll have to ease up —but now comes the question—would I rather take a chance by ignoring this so that almost certainly I die in harness? Or shall I take it easy? It sounds boring, but I admit I'm tired—"

Well, he'd ignored the warning—but now it became clear from his entries that a mood of perplexity assailed him. Just two days before he had written that letter to Eleanor, he had written much the same thing in his diary—and he had added that Jervis Singleton was get-ting rather impatient for a decision. Eleanor's mouth tightened when she read that. To her it sounded as if the younger man had recognised the frailty of the one and had deliberately played on it—

"No, I don't like him," Eleanor told herself. "He's

ruthless—honestly, how could I work with him? It just wouldn't do! I'll have to turn the idea down—"

Yet, after one particularly gruelling session with Mr. Franklin, she wasn't so sure. Despite the introduction of several new and charming lines, their profits had dropped steadily over the last two years.

"And that despite the fact that you've been singularly free from strikes," Mr. Franklin pointed out.

"Yes, but why?" Eleanor wanted to know.

Mr. Franklin shrugged his shoulders.

"Less money available for luxuries these days," he reminded her. "Particularly when it's a case of breakable articles.

"Yes, I suppose so," Eleanor sighed, and frowned. "I do wish we knew how Stapleton's have come through the same period."

"That would certainly be a very useful piece of information," Mr. Franklin agreed. "But unfortunately quite unobtainable."

"Yes, I suppose so," Eleanor replied. And then, as the thought suddenly occurred to her : "Mr. Franklin, I suppose it's equally impossible that Stapleton's should know just what our financial position is?"

Mr. Franklin looked at her sharply.

"What makes you ask that, Miss Chalfont?"

"Just that it seems to me a little strange that this suggestion has come from Stapleton's just when our turnover has dropped," Eleanor explained. "Of course, there may be nothing in it, but it is something of a coincidence, don't you think?"

"Yes, perhaps," Mr. Franklin agreed. "Though really one has very little to go on. Indeed, the one thing I can state positively is that had your trade figures improved, or even merely been held, I'm quite sure that Mr. Simon would have dismissed the idea immediately and finally."

"Yes, there would have been nothing really for us to have gained from a merger," Eleanor agreed thoughtfully. "And I can't help feeling that whether they knew before making the suggestion just how things were with us or not, they are sufficiently astute to have picked up from the fact that Uncle Simon didn't turn them straight down that things aren't quite as good as they were."

Mr. Franklin considered this for a few moments before he replied.

"I don't think you can regard that as a certainty. But as a probability, yes. It depends on how deep an understanding they had of your uncle's character. Or perhaps I should say—how deep an understanding *he* had?"

"You mean—it's the son, Jervis Stapleton, who is the prime mover in this?" she asked quickly, and he nodded.

"That is the opinion your uncle had, and I believe it to be the correct one though, of course, the father must have agreed. But none the less, a very great deal depends on the son's character and mentality. You've met him, haven't you, Miss Chalfont? So what's your opinion of him? Forceful? Intelligent? Able to see any other point of view than his own? What do you think?"

What did she think? Eleanor was not too sure.

"You must remember that the circumstances on the few occasions that I've met him didn't make it very easy for me to make a balanced judgment," she said slowly. "But—forceful, yes, that, certainly. As for being intelligent—" she bit her lip reflectively. "He was pretty shrewd over working out that something must have happened to Uncle that morning—for what that's worth. But as for seeing any other point of view than his own—I should think that's very doubtful. At least, he might see it and make use of it to suit himself, but I very much doubt if he'd ever change his own mind on some-one else's account."

"Not withstanding the circumstances of your meeting, you seem to have formed a pretty detailed impression of the young man," Mr. Franklin said drily. "Well, if what you say is right, it would seem that you will not find it very pleasant to work with him."

"I know. I've thought of that," Eleanor confessed. "And judging by the correspondence between Staple-ton's and Uncle Simon, they have rather seemed to take it for granted that they'd be the senior partner of any new firm. So, dealing with a woman, I think it would be almost impossible for me—for us to get a fair deal."

"I see," Mr. Franklin regarded her thoughtfully.

"I'm wondering if, all things considered, it might not be worth while considering selling outright," Eleanor told him quietly.

"Yes, I can see that's bound to have occurred to you in the circumstances," Mr. Franklin admitted. "Whether it would be wise or not, only events could show. I wouldn't like to give an opinion. I can only tell you that, so far as I know, your uncle never considered taking such a course."

"No? But then his circumstances and mine are so very different," Eleanor pointed out. "He was a man, he had devoted his whole adult life to the firm and wouldn't want to surrender his entire interest if it could be avoided. And, most important of all, he had no other interests in life."

"The family—" Mr. Franklin began, but Eleanor shook her head.

"His interest in his family was to some extent, at least, a question of how the various members of it affected the firm. I, as you probably know, Mr. Franklin, am engaged to be married in three months' time. I want to make a real home for my husband and later on, for our children. I don't believe I can do that properly if I've got the burden of the firm on my shoulders."

"So you would sacrifice the firm—"

"Hardly that, Mr. Franklin," Eleanor said steadily. "But there is such a thing as getting one's priorities in the right order. That's what I'm determined to do. And that's why I'm considering the possibility of selling out."

"H'm. Well, I see your point, Miss Chalfont, but there may be difficulties ahead. For one thing, although Mr. Edgar's holding in the firm is small when compared to yours, he could none the less hold up proceedings if he refused to sell, as, I must warn you, I think he might. Particularly as, whether Stapleton's have any idea of how Chalfont's are placed at present financially, they will certainly have to know before they make a definite offer. And it doesn't help matters that there will be heavy death duties to pay—" He considered for a moment. "You haven't heard from Stapleton's about this since your uncle's death?"

"No, I haven't," Eleanor admitted. "But they'd surely realise that I must be very busy and that in any case, I've got to master all the details of this possible transaction before I make a decision. But about one thing I'm determined, Mr. Franklin. *I* am not going to approach them about it. If they are still interested in a merger, they must get in touch with me."

"They will," Mr. Franklin said positively. "Well, good luck, whatever you decide, Miss Chalfont. You'll keep me informed of any developments, won't you?"

"Yes, I will," Eleanor promised.

*   *   *

The more Eleanor delved into the affairs of the firm and in particular, into the correspondence between Stapleton's and her uncle, the more she felt that Geoff had been right. A merger, with herself as the senior representative of Chalfont's, simply wouldn't work, for the reasons she had given Mr. Franklin.

"It's the only way," she told herself. "But Uncle Edgar won't like it—still, if he had a bigger share of the price we got than his holding really warrants, it might be all right. After all, though he's not as old as Uncle Simon was, he must be thinking of retiring, and this would mean he could do it in greater comfort—"

Yes, it really was the only thing to do. The only bother was that Stapleton's made no attempt to get in touch with her, and with her chin set obstinately, she told herself that if they thought she was coming begging to them, they were mistaken—

Then, out of the blue, she had a telephone call from Jervis Stapleton. He came straight to the point.

"I imagine, by now, that you are aware of our suggestion of a merger with Chalfont's," he began coolly.

"Yes, that is so, Mr. Stapleton," Eleanor agreed as coolly though her heart was racing. This was it!

"With all the other business which you must attend to, we appreciate that you may not yet have come to a decision," Jervis went on. "And we have no wish to hustle you—"

"I appreciate that," Eleanor said smoothly. But if he didn't want to hustle her, what was he ringing up for?

"What we would like, however," Jervis went on as if he was fully aware of what was in her mind, "is that as well as considering the possibility of a merger between our two firms, you would also consider another possibility—"

"Yes, Mr. Stapleton?" Eleanor asked a little breathlessly.

"Yes, Miss Chalfont. The possibility that you should sell outright to us."

CHAPTER IV

ELEANOR snatched the telephone from her ear and stared at it as if it had bitten her.

That Jervis should have made such a suggestion just at the very time when she had come to the conclusion that such a course was the only sensible one to take was the most disconcerting thing that had ever happened to her. It was as if he not only had the ability to calculate the way in which her mind would work, but had also instinctively known the psychological moment to strike.

"Hallo?" His voice rattled in the earpiece. "Are you still there, Miss Chalfont?"

"Oh—yes, I'm still here," Eleanor told him. "But I must admit, rendered just rather breathless by your suggestion!"

"Oh?" he said coolly. "Hadn't the idea occurred to you?"

Of course, he would make a direct question of it! As if she was going to admit it! If ever there was a time to play hard to get, this was it! But it would be no use telling him a direct lie. Even over the telephone, when he was unable to see her face, she'd never be able to convince him.

"Oh yes," she said as coolly. "It's already been suggested to me, but, naturally, it's out of the question!"

And even as she spoke the words, she was convinced

of their truth. It was one thing to have had the idea herself, quite another now that he had shown his hand. Indeed, she wondered how on earth she could have considered it for a single moment.

"Oh? Why?"

Of course, the answer to that was simple enough.

"Because, since you're suggesting it, you think you'd make more out of it than we would!"

But that was the sort of thing it was wiser to leave unsaid. So, instead, she laughed softly.

"My dear Mr. Stapleton, isn't that rather an ingenuous question?" she suggested. But if she had hoped to abash him, she was mistaken.

"I don't think so. But please do tell me why you do." Well, he'd asked for it!

"Because, for one thing, it's a family business in which we naturally take a pride," she snapped. "If you can understand that!"

"You mean you regard it as something more than a profit-making machine?" he suggested. "Well, that, believe it or not, is something I do understand. I've the same feeling about our set-up. But one has to be practical—"

"Of course," Eleanor agreed warily as he paused.

"Well, you speak of it as a family affair," he explained with an air of overdone patience which indicated that she ought to be able to work this one out for herself. "But I rather doubt that. With one exception, I'd say most of your family regard the firm as a money-making concern only. No, with perhaps two exceptions."

"And who are they?" Eleanor asked, holding her anger in check with considerable difficulty.

"Your aunt, Miss Helen Chalfont, who obviously has little or no interest in the firm from any point of view," he said unhesitatingly. "And of course, Mr. Edgar Chalfont. Now he really is heart and soul devoted to the firm and its well-being."

"Aren't you forgetting someone else?" Eleanor suggested drily.

"No, I don't think so," he replied consideringly. "Your mother, Mrs. Edgar and the twins regard it simply as a milch cow which exists purely to give them their particular sort of good time—"

That was so true that Eleanor could not contradict him.

"You're still forgetting one person," she insisted. "Myself!"

"Ah yes," Jervis said slowly. "You. But then you, so I understand, will be getting married in the near future. Won't it be something of a problem to run a home and be a career woman at one and the same time?"

Really, he was outrageous! To probe into her personal affairs like this and expect her to confide in him!

"I'm afraid your outlook is rather dated, Mr. Stapleton," deliberately she infused a mild amusement into her voice. "Many women combine the two quite successfully, and I really don't see why I shouldn't do the same thing!"

"H'm! And what does your fiancé think about it?"

That really was going too far, and she told him so in no uncertain words.

"So now I know just where I get off," he commented when finally she came to a halt. "But, Miss Chalfont, I know something else as well now!"

"I'm afraid I'm not interested—"

"No, but I am. It's simply this—there's far too much of the eternal female in you for you ever to be a really successful business woman! A pity. I'd hoped for something different from you!"

Without answering, Eleanor rang off. The impertinence of the man! She fumed furiously for several moments. Whatever she might have thought before this conversation nothing, she was determined, should now persuade her to fall in with his wishes—

The telephone bell rang again. Eleanor lifted it.

"Eleanor Chalfont speaking," she said crisply.

"And still rather out at elbows with the world," suggested that now familiar and hateful voice. "Well, not surprising, really. I've realised I do owe you an apology, Miss Chalfont."

"I think you do," Eleanor agreed. And, of course, it was true. None the less, she crossed her fingers. Her contact with Jervis had been of the slightest, but she was reasonably sure that he wasn't the sort of man who would bring himself to make an apology unless, of course, he hoped to gain by it.

"Yes," he went on with apparent gravity, "I was in too much of a hurry to make my proposition. I should have given you longer to get used to it! And instead of discussing it over the telephone in this disembodied manner, we should have done so in more pleasant circumstances. Will you have dinner with me some night soon, Miss Chalfont?"

"No, I will not!" Eleanor said furiously. "And I'll be glad if you will please understand—"

"You're not by any chance afraid, are you?" he interrupted, unmistakable mockery in his voice.

"Afraid? Of what?" she asked truculently.

"Oh, that in such circumstances—dim lights, soft music and—all the rest of it—"

"Such as you exercising your no doubt considerable charm?" Eleanor returned the mockery with interest. "No, Mr. Stapleton, I'm not afraid that any of those things will make me change my mind."

"No? I'd find that statement far more convincing if you'd accept my invitation," he challenged.

"Ah yes, but then you see it might really be nearer the truth if I admitted that I'm afraid of one thing," Eleanor told him with deceptive gentleness. "And that is—I should so very likely be bored!"

But Jervis, far from being quelled, roared with laughter.

"Well, despite that nasty crack, I'll be generous and confess that I know I shouldn't be! You would, I feel sure, be a most stimulating companion!"

"Thank you, kind sir!" Eleanor mocked. "To have received such a flattering compliment as that from you goes some way to changing my opinion of you!"

"Then won't you give me the opportunity of completely changing it?" he coaxed. "I really would do my best not to bore you!"

Eleanor hesitated. It was perhaps fortunate that Jervis could not see the litle dimple that flickered momentarily at the corner of her mouth or the glint of mischief in her dark eyes. He might have realised that she had every intention of taking up the challenge he had thrown down perhaps more obviously than he had intended.

"Very well, Mr. Stapleton. On those terms, I accept your invitation with every intention of doing my share to make it an occasion we both remember!"

"I'm sure you will, Miss Chalfont!" He sounded amused, but she thought she caught an alert note in his voice as if he realised—and accepted—the significance of what she had said. "Now, when would suit you? Some time this week? Wednesday or Thursday?"

"Thursday," Eleanor said promptly. "I already have an engagement for Wednesday."

"Which good manners will, of course, prevent you from cutting."

"Well, yes, of course, but that's not my only reason, Mr. Stapleton," Eleanor explained smoothly. "My fiancé and I are going out together, so naturally, I don't *want* to cut it!"

"Naturally," Jervis agreed as smoothly. "Thursday, then. May I come along to Kingsworthy House at, say, seven o'clock to pick you up?"

"Thank you," Eleanor accepted the offer graciously. "I hope you will have time to have a drink with my mother before we leave?"

"Yes, indeed," Jervis said politely. "I shall look forward to that!"

"Good! Then until Thursday, Mr. Stapleton. Oh, just one thing. Mother and I live in the West Pavilion—"

"Oh, but I remember that, Miss Chalfont," Jervis said softly. "You see, anything to do with you is of importance to me!"

Eleanor laid the telephone down smartly in its cradle. She had had enough!

"Of all the conceited, self-opinionated, pig-headed men, he's the worst I've ever met!" she told herself vehemently. Then the dimple flickered again. Yes, he was all those things, but for that very reason, it promised to be an exciting evening—and what a feather in her cap it was going to be making him acknowledge that he had not got the better of her!

She drew a deep, quivering breath of anticipation.

Soft music, dim lights, charm—he would find they didn't get him anywhere! It really was going to be fun!

*　　*　　*

Eleanor told only two people of Jervis's invitation—her mother and Geoff. Both were equally surprised, but whereas Kitty easily accepted the explanation that it was difficult for either of them to have an uninterrupted interview during office hours, and went on to discuss what Eleanor should wear, Geoff was not so easily satisfied.

"Whose idea was it?" he demanded, and when Eleanor told him he nodded, tight-lipped. "I thought so! And from his point of view, a sound move. But for the life of me, I can't understand why you fell for that line of talk."

"If by 'that line of talk' you mean that he thinks it will be easier to get round me in pleasant, informal circumstances than in either of our offices, then you're as wrong as he is," Eleanor said drily. "I haven't fallen for it—I'm neither so vain nor so silly! But while I do think you ought to have realised that, I rather hope he doesn't because—two can play at that game!"

"Hey, just what do you mean by that?" Geoff asked sharply. "Because if you mean what it sounds like to me, I'm not having it!"

"Oh, Geoff!" Eleanor protested, more impatiently than she realised. "All I mean is that he may find *he* is the one to be influenced by the informality of the occasion. And if so, it may be easier for me to find out the truth than if we faced one another across an office desk!"

"Shouldn't bank on that, if I were you," Geoff advised. "Judging by the little I've seen of him—and the very much more I've heard about him—I very much doubt he'd lose his head no matter how pretty and beguiling a girl might be!"

"Geoff, that's beastly of you," Eleanor flashed, her colour rising. "Beguiling—how horrible! I'd no such idea in my mind, believe me!"

Geoff regarded her unsmilingly.

"I admit it doesn't line up with what I've always felt you to be," he said sombrely. "But then, since your uncle died, you haven't been very much like yourself, have you?"

"Of course I have," Eleanor protested, near tears. "Why should I change just because—"

"Just because now you've suddenly got both money and power?" Geoff finished for her. "It's been known to change people before now, you know."

"Yes, I do know," Eleanor admitted with a sigh. "And in a way, you're right, Geoff. I have changed. I don't mean it's made me feel full of my own importance, or made me enjoy being in a position to give orders. I'd be happy about it all if I felt like that. And I'm *not* happy, Geoff. I feel as if all the cares in the world were on my shoulders, and I don't think I'm the right sort of person to be in that sort of position."

"Well, you know what I suggested—sell out to Stapleton's," Geoff reminded her, but Eleanor shook her head.

"Somehow I can't feel that's the right thing to do," she told him. "And you see, Geoff, that's just the trouble. I don't want to have all this power—but I've too much sense of responsibility just to throw it on one side. Besides—" she stopped short of the brink of telling Geoff that Jervis had suggested just the same course and that it was on this account that she was determined to maintain Chalfont's independence. Fortunately, Geoff misunderstood the significance of that final word.

"Besides, you feel that because your uncle has wished this on to you, and now he's dead, it wouldn't be fair or right not to do as he wished?" he suggested. "That's a lot of nonsense, Eleanor. From what you've told me, he himself was in two minds what to do, and after all, he did tell you that you'd got a completely free hand—"

"I know," Eleanor sighed. "And that's just what makes it so difficult. He left me no guidance—I've got to do this entirely off my own bat?"

"Well, fair enough!" Geoff said impatiently. "Why, in those circumstances, should you take it for granted that the right thing for you to do is of a necessity the one that is against your own personal interests? And it's going to be, Eleanor, if you let yourself be permanently lumbered with this infernal firm, because I don't see how it's possible for you to combine marriage and a career like this one will be! And you'd better get it quite clear in your mind, Eleanor, I'm not willing to have a part-time wife! Do you understand?"

"But that's just why Uncle Simon wanted us to put off getting married for a year," she reminded him. "By then—"

"By then you'll be so completely enmeshed in the job that it'll be harder than ever to get free of it," Geoff interrupted grimly. "No, Eleanor, you've got to choose —and not waste any time about it. Either we get married at the end of August as we planned or—" He stopped short, biting his lips. "Oh, Eleanor, I'm hating this! And I hadn't meant to say any more that what I had done on the day of your uncle's funeral. But it doesn't seem to have made any impression on you, and I can only see disillusion and heartbreak ahead for both of us if you go ahead with being a big business woman!" He paused, evidently expecting some reply from her, but when it didn't come he went on deliberately: "I'm going to be absolutely honest with you, Eleanor. I know myself for the sort of bloke who doesn't really grow up until he's got a wife and, later, children depending on him. Maybe it's an old-fashioned point of view, and these days, I expect a lot of women would say it isn't fair to expect a woman just to stick at home and do the chores. But there's more to it than that! It's—" he stopped short and shook his head. "No, it's no use. If you can't see for yourself, I don't think it's any good me trying to explain."

"But I do see," Eleanor said earnestly. "Honestly I do, Geoff. And I've never wanted anything more than to make a home for us—"

"Yet you had every intention of keeping on with working after we were married, even before this blew up," he pointed out.

"Yes, but only for a time. Just until—"

"Until I showed signs of being able to give you the comforts you've always been used to," Geoff suggested bitterly. "You've never really regarded me as being a good risk, have you? Never quite trusted me to look after you—that's why you've always planned to have an extra life-line in the form of your own job. And why you won't give up now!"

She protested that it was not true—and Geoff believed her—or wanted to believe her so much that he convinced himself that he did. And Eleanor promised that, once she had seen Jervis and heard what he had to say, she would find some way of evading the responsibility which had been so inexorably thrust upon her.

Yet, later, wondering just what that way could be, she found herself forced to admit that there had been something in what Geoff had said. Deeply though she loved him, the idea of them relying entirely on what he earned had never entered her head. She had just taken it for granted that she would keep on working. So many girls did, after they were married. Why shouldn't she? As simple as that. But it wasn't, really.

There was something missing in their relationship although it was only now that she realised it. Had she known beyond all doubt that he was stronger than she was, how different it might have been—how much easier to deal with the problem Uncle Simon had left her!

And yet no sooner had the idea formulated in her mind than she rejected it.

"I don't want Geoff to be any different from what he is!" she told herself firmly. "I know they say that at heart a woman wants to know she's met her master in the man she marries, but I don't believe it! A man like that who was always making one feel inferior would be impossible to live with. I know I'd never fall for one of that sort!"

*   *   *

Simon had been so frank about his dislike of mourning that none of the family had even considered wearing it once the funeral was over. Consequently, Eleanor had all her wardrobe to choose from for her outing with Jervis. Unfortunately this didn't altogether help for he had not said where he intended taking her for dinner, and though it would have been sensible to ring him up and ask, Eleanor couldn't bring herself to do so.

Finally she settled on a sleeveless greenish-blue dress

of wild silk which had a short matching jacket. Without the jacket, it easily passed muster as a cocktail dress; with it, just as a pretty dress one might wear at almost any time of day. Because the last few days had been chilly after dark, she borrowed her mother's fur cape and, at Kitty's suggestion, a spray of gold leaves to wear on her shoulder.

"It just gives you a finish—a sort of sparkle," Kitty explained. And though Eleanor wasn't at all sure that she wanted to sparkle for Jervis's benefit, she had to admit that her mother was right. It was the finishing touch.

Jervis arrived punctually at seven o'clock. Eleanor was quick to notice that he was wearing a lounge suit which not only made her congratulate herself on her own choice of dress, but made it clear that they were not going to anywhere very sophisticated. Well, of course, he wouldn't choose anywhere like that. This wasn't, after all, a social occasion in the true sense. Simply they wanted somewhere quiet to discuss business.

That being so, she rather wished that her mother wouldn't make it so very evident how much she was enjoying the presence of a personable male, both by listening to whatever he might say with such flattering attention, and then by asking him, rather wistfully, to pour out the drinks.

"I do hope you don't mind, but somehow it does seem to me to be essentially a man's job, though of course—" with a shrug and a soft little sigh—"I've had to get used to doing it for myself for a good many years now!"

And that made Eleanor feel uncomfortable, too. To ask, in effect, for sympathy from this of all men went against the grain. But Jervis, she had to admit, took the situation in his stride.

"I quite agree with you," he said pleasantly. "It is a man's job, and I'm only too glad to be able to relieve you of it."

Kitty sighed, this time pleasurably.

"You know, I've an idea, Mr. Stapleton, that you are one of those rare men who feel it's natural for a woman to turn to them for help," she said pensively. "All the more delightful to meet, these days, because it's a type that on seldom comes across."

"Is it?" Jervis handed Kitty her glass and then presented Eleanor with hers. "I wonder if that's because we feel that such an attitude wouldn't be welcome these days in a good many quarters? What do you think, Miss Chalfont? Did courtesy go out of fashion when equality for women came in? Does she prefer rights to privileges?" His dark eyes met hers provocatively.

Of course Eleanor had known all along that he had challenged her to a duel this evening; that each of them would be on their guard, anxious to find each other's weakness without revealing their own. But to try to provoke her like this into a display of resentment in front of her mother wasn't playing the game. Well, she'd show him that though she recognised his jibe for what it was, he had missed his target entirely.

"But is it a question of rights or privileges?" she asked blandly. "Isn't it just a matter of good manners? And I really don't see how they can ever be out of date! After all, it's just a matter of common sense, don't you think, whether it's a social or a business occasion. Rudeness—and crudeness—rarely get one anywhere!"

There was a moment's silence. Then, very slightly, Jervis lifted his glass to her, silently acknowledging that he had taken her point.

Shortly after, they left. Their recent little skirmish may have been in the minds of both of them for Jervis handed Eleanor into the front seat of his car with, surely more than normal punctiliousness while Eleanor's thanks were equally formal.

But once they were on their way, Eleanor found to her surprise that she felt pleasurably relaxed. Jervis was an extremely good driver, neither over cautious nor too reckless, but smoothly alert to every situation.

He drove in silence, and Eleanor, who herself preferred not to talk when driving, respected his feelings until, suddenly, she realised that instead of going into Kingswell as she had taken it for granted would be the case, Jervis was taking the ring road which encircled it and which, so far as Eleanor knew, did not lead to anywhere that they could dine at.

"Where are we going?" she asked with a sharpness which might have excused Jervis from thinking that there was apprehension as well. If that was so, it apparently amused him for she saw that his well cut lips curved into a smile.

"To my home," he explained simply. "Or, I suppose I should say, to my parents' home. Why? Did you think I was planning to elope with you or something?"

"Of course not!" Eleanor denied indignantly. "Simply, you hadn't said where you were taking me and I had assumed it would be somewhere in Kingswell."

"I did consider that," he admitted, slowing a little to allow an impatient driver in a sports car to pass him. "Silly fool!" he commented angrily. "With a dangerous curve that's clearly signposted coming, he must put on speed! They ask for it, some of these drivers—and, unfortunately, involve others who aren't to blame. As I was saying, I did consider a hotel or a restaurant, but then it occurred to me that really, we could talk in greater comfort and privacy at my home—I do hope you don't mind?"

She did mind—very much! Whether it was true or not that this plan was a matter of second thoughts she didn't know, but it was certainly a clever move! At a hotel or restaurant, they would have met on equal terms. In his home, he would be absolutely at his ease while she, not only a stranger but very much in the minority among people who had been her family's rivals for years, would of a necessity be at a disadvantage.

"Not at all," she said coolly. "I quite see what you mean. And it will be delightful to meet your family in less formal circumstances than has hitherto been the case."

"I hope—I think you will find it so," he replied, and went on with what sounded like genuine feeling: "I like my family, and it's not just because blood is thicker than water. I feel I'd have chosen them for friends even if we hadn't been related. And that, I gather, is not a common state of affairs."

There might have been a note of interrogation in his final remark, but if so, Eleanor ignored it.

"Oh, I should think it varies a great deal," she said

vaguely. "I mean, a blood tie can mean that people have a lot in common or it can mean the very reverse. After all, think how many ancestors have contributed to our personalities!"

"Yes, indeed," he said abstractedly, and slowing down, turned down a side road. A little way along he entered a gateway which led to the crescent sweep of a gravel drive.

It was still broad daylight, and as she got out of the car, Eleanor looked at the house with considerable curiosity. Until this moment she had had no idea in what sort of house the Stapleton family lived, but if she had given the matter any thought, she would probably have taken it for granted that they would naturally choose something very new and very obviously expensive. She could not have been more wrong.

Jervis's home was Georgian, of just about the same period as Kingsworthy House, she thought, though considerably smaller, but what it lacked in size it made up for in simple elegance. There was none of that top-heavy look that Kingsworthy had.

"How very lovely!" she exclaimed involuntarily.

"So I think," Jervis said softly, his eyes wandering with appreciation over the beautiful façade now glowing in the early evening sunshine. "I never get tired of it—it's the perfection of its proportions, of course. A lovely period. One of the richest, if not the very richest, we've ever known. But come along in—the inside, if anything, is even better."

With complete informality he opened the front door with his latchkey and ushered her into the white wood panelled hall. As he followed her in, a door opened and Mrs. Stapleton came out.

She and Jervis were strikingly alike in appearance so that even if Eleanor had never met her, she would have recognised them as mother and son. There was the same well shaped, well poised head, the same strong facial lines, though in Mrs. Stapleton's case they were softened not only because they were a feminine version of Jervis's but also because she had achieved a tranquillity which he, so far, had not. There was a warmth, too, in her manner which suggested that she was not afraid to show her feelings.

"Here we are, Mother," Jervis said easily. "Absolutely on time, I'd have you note!"

"My dear, I'm delighted to welcome you," Mrs. Stapleton said kindly, taking Eleanor's hand in a pleasantly firm grasp. "Jervis, take Miss Chalfont's fur to my little sitting room, and then join us in the drawing room. This way, Miss Chalfont!"

There were two people in the drawing room whose long, open windows framed a picture of a beautifully kept garden. One was Jervis's father, the other, his married sister, Dora Vance, a pretty dark-haired girl about Eleanor's age or perhaps a little older.

When greetings had been exchanged, Mr. Stapleton suggested a pre-dinner drink, and was pouring them out when Jervis came in.

He greeted his father with a gentle touch on the shoulder and saluted his sister with a grin and a quick hug.

"Nice to see you, Dodie," he commented. "But where's John?"

"Held up with a talkative client," Dodie explained with a grimace. "But he phoned through to say he's shaken him off now and he'll be here any moment."

"And my niece and nephew?" Jervis asked, taking the glasses his father had filled and handing them round.

"Dying to see Uncle Jervis—in fact, you're booked to go up and say goodnight to them before dinner—and give an exhibition of penny-vanishing!"

Jervis groaned and turned to Eleanor.

"The last time the infants were staying here, I rashly did that trick of apparently laying a penny on their heads, giving it a good rub and then producing it out of their mouths. It was all too popular, particularly as they stuck to the pennies! Oh well, I asked for it!"

"You did," Dodie agreed cheerfully. "And as a result, they now regard you as their number one uncle—in other words you've hoodwinked those poor infants into thinking you're something out of the ordinary with no more than a skilful bit of sleight of hand! Immoral, I call it!"

There was a very brief silence—Eleanor thought she heard Mrs. Stapleton catch her breath. Then John Vance arrived, and in the little stir that caused, the earlier conversation was forgotten.

Later, a school-age brother and sister turned up, and then, with a glance at the clock, Mrs. Stapleton suggested that if Jervis was going to say goodnight to the children, he'd better go now or he'd hold up dinner.

Jervis, his sister and brother-in-law put down their glasses and stood up. Then, just as they were moving over to the door, John turned to Eleanor who, to his eyes, looked a little out of it.

"Won't you come as well, Miss Chalfont?" he suggested pleasantly. "They're jolly little kids, though I suppose I ought not to say so!"

"I'd love to come," Eleanor said quickly, and meant it, though she didn't quite understand why. Perhaps because she was curious. Perhaps because, on a visit to the nursery, there would be no formal conversation as there would be in the drawing room—

There was a shriek of delight as the four grown-ups came into the nursery. Two small pyjama-clad figures hurled themselves out of bed and bestowed their kisses with complete impartiality on their father and uncle. In their exuberance, even Eleanor came in for a share.

Then the penny trick had to be performed, and Eleanor noticed that Jervis had taken the trouble to provide himself with bright new pennies.

·John had to tell a story, evidently a serial one, for it seemed to have no particular beginning. It concerned the adventures of two children—obviously the two who were listening so intently—who were wrecked on a desert island.

Suddenly the sound of the gong boomed through the house. John brought the narrative to a hurried conclusion and the four of them went downstairs.

"Wuff!" Jervis commented, smoothing his dark hair. "A pleasant experience, but an exhausting one!"

"You'd say that, old man, if you had it every night!" John told him feelingly.

Dodie laughed.

"You know perfectly well you wouldn't miss it for anything!" she said, linking her arm through his.

The dining room was as pleasant a room in its way as the drawing room, though not so large. It was impossible not to notice how beautifully and suitably both rooms were furnished, yet without the effect of turning either into a stiff period piece.

The meal was excellent, too—simple English food, beautifully cooked and attractively presented. It was quite impossible not to enjoy it, as Eleanor quickly found.

It was a pleasant meal in another respect as well. It was served at a round table—Eleanor found herself placed between her host and John Vance—so conversation was general rather than to one's immediate neighbours. It was general in topic as well so that though, occasionally, a family matter might be briefly mentioned, in the main, Eleanor was not left out and found herself taking part quite naturally.

It was not until they were half way through the meal, when Jervis and Dodie were sparring amiably over something, that a disconcerting idea occurred to Eleanor so suddenly that she stopped short in the middle of a sentence.

This scene in which she was taking part was so perfectly staged as to be unreal.

Oh yes, it was a beautiful home, and no doubt they were nice people in their way, but they were Stapletons, none the less. Out for themselves. Out to present themselves to her, especially Jervis, in as favourable a light as possible.

Well, why be surprised? Wasn't it just what she had guessed was his reason for bringing her here? But she had thought it was because he felt he would be more at ease than she would and would so have the advantage. Now she realised that his mind worked in a more subtle way than that.

She was deliberately being put too much at her ease—compelled to relax in this happy family setting—to see Jervis as a warm-hearted individual rather than a shrewd business man.

She drew a deep breath. No, not just shrewd. That was altogether too weak a description.

Jervis Stapleton was a really dangerous man.

CHAPTER V

FOR the rest of the meal, Eleanor found it very difficult to join naturally in the conversation until she
noticed that more than once glances that might have
expressed perplexity or conveyed a warning were being
exchanged between members of the Stapleton family.
After that, she forced herself to take part, though not,
she felt, altogether convincingly. When the last course
was finished and they returned to the drawing room for
coffee and liqueurs, Eleanor was sure that she was not
the only person who was glad to break from that confin-
ing circle dictated by the shape of the table.

Only Jervis, she noticed resentfully, seemed completely at his ease though he was perfectly well aware
that others weren't. Why else did he suggest to his
younger brother that he should put on a record of *Swan
Lake* suitably subdued to make pleasant background
music or, if anyone didn't want to talk, an excuse for
remaining silent?

When, perhaps half an hour later, a maid came in
to remove the coffee trolley, the school-age brother and
sister vanished silently from the room. Then, when the
end of a topic of conversation came, Mr. and Mrs.
Stapleton excused themselves with the explanation of a
committee meeting they both had to attend.

Now only Dodie and John Vance were left, and
Eleanor wondered if it was because they weren't so
experienced as the older couple were at this sort of
thing—or was it, she thought ironically, that it had all
been decided beforehand? Did they think it would be
less alarming to her than if they rushed out in a crowd
with the obvious intent of giving Jervis a clear field?

Once again, were they trying to give her a false sense of ease?

At last the Vances went and Eleanor could not repress a soft little chuckle. Apparently surprised, Jervis looked at her questioningly.

"Only that it rather reminded me of a play," Eleanor explained demurely. "When everybody fades discreetly from the stage leaving the two principal characters alone together for their big scene!"

Jervis laughed appreciatively.

"Yes, perhaps there is some similarity," he agreed, but went on deliberately: "Though I seem to remember when that happens in a play, it's usually in order to give Hugo or Roderick, or whatever his name may be, an opportunity of making a proposal of marriage to the lady of his choice—something I hadn't planned to do—yet," he finished outrageously. "I feel it's just rather too soon, you see!"

Was he just tormenting her? Was he deliberately trying to make her feel rather foolish? Or was he himself feeling a little foolish that she had so easily seen through his tactics and was trying to disguise the fact? She didn't know—and really, it didn't matter so long as she didn't let him labour under the misapprehension that he had scored off her in any way.

"Too soon?" She looked at him with raised brows. "Don't you mean—too late?" And, dreamy-eyed, she glanced down at Geoff's shining ring. Then, abruptly, in as crisp and businesslike a voice as she could contrive: "Shall we come to the point, Mr. Stapleton? I'm quite sure you're going to produce what are to you entirely convincing reasons why our firms should either amalgamate or I should sell out to you—and that's what you would really prefer should happen, isn't it?"

"It is," he agreed unhesitatingly, but his eyes were very wary, and Eleanor felt a little stab of exultation. She had contrived, in the setting which *he* had chosen, to wrest the initiative from him, and now she had deliberately taken the war into the enemy's country. The advantage was hers—and she had every intention of keeping it.

"Before you try to convince me that either course

would be to Chalfont's advantage, there are two questions I'd like to ask you," she told him.

"By all means," Jervis said equably, and waited politely for her to speak.

"The first is—on this question of selling out to you," Eleanor explained. "Did you ever make such a suggestion to my uncle?"

"No, I didn't," Jervis replied with convincing promptness.

"Then why make it to me?" Eleanor asked quickly.

"Oh!" Jervis's hands moved expressively and for the first time Eleanor was aware that he was growing impatient with what, no doubt, he felt to be her stupidity. "It would have been waste of time! Chalfont's was your uncle's one interest in life. A merger he might—I would be inclined to say he *would* have agreed to in time. A complete relinquishment of what was not only his work, but also his hobby—never. So I didn't waste my time suggesting it."

Eleanor nodded without comment. She thought Jervis was quite clever enough to have made that assessment of Uncle Simon's character, and in any case, that he had not suggested a complete take-over was clear from what Uncle Simon had said in his letter. None the less, she didn't feel quite satisfied. She realised that Jervis was speaking again.

"But I think it's only fair that I should tell you that in view of Mr. Chalfont's age and poor health, I had hoped that he might find, Stapleton though I am, that he could trust me to carry the lion's share of the burden—"

"That's very frank of you, Mr. Stapleton," Eleanor said very softly. "But really, isn't it just another way of saying that you hoped to get exactly what you wanted —complete control—with none of the outlay of capital that you would have to make now that I'm in control?"

"Yes, no doubt one could put it that way," Jervis agreed judicially. "But you must remember, Miss Chalfont, that in such circumstances, your uncle would still have been a partner in the combined firm, even if a sleeping one. And that would have meant that he would have continued to draw money from the firm although he was doing little or nothing to earn it. Do I make my-self clear?"

"Oh, perfectly," Eleanor said shortly, furious with herself for not seeing the trap she had given him the opportunity of setting for her. She ought to have rea-lised that such a display of frankness was too good to be true! And now he had got the initiative again—

"And your other question, Miss Chalfont?" he asked after a moment or two's silence.

"Oh—yes," Eleanor said hurriedly. "This is something quite different. I'm curious to know how the question of a merger became common gossip before you and Uncle Simon had reached any sort of agreement!"

"What?" There was no doubt about it, she had startled him now! "Are you quite sure?"

"Oh, quite," she assured him positively. "I heard it from two sources—from my mother, who heard it spoken of at the hairdressers, and from my fiancé, who was asked if he knew anything about it at the King's Head."

Jervis's face was very grim and his fingers tapped restlessly on the arm of his chair.

"Can you remember exactly when they mentioned the matter to you?" he asked curtly.

"Oh yes. On the day that Uncle Simon—died—he sent a message to me by Manning, his personal attend-ant, to ask me to go and see him before leaving from the office as, so he told me a little later, he was waiting for a telephone call—yours."

"Yes," Jervis nodded. "Well?"

"When I came down from seeing him, my mother called me into her room. She asked me if it was true about the merger."

"And you said—?"

"That it wasn't—I didn't know anything about it until after Uncle's death," Eleanor explained. "He left me a long letter—"

"We will discuss that in a moment or two," Jervis said brusquely. "Now, your fiancé—?"

"When I went out to the stables to get my car, I ex-changed a few words with him. And he asked me the same question—was there any truth in the story."

Jervis got up and paced up and down the room a few times before he replied.

"This is a complete surprise to me, Miss Chalfont," he told her, coming to a halt in front of her chair. "On our side, I would have said that only my father, my mother and myself knew we were going to make this approach to you. My parents——" he smiled fleetingly. "I would answer both for their integrity and their good sense as I would my own—if that's much of a guarantee to you. But seriously, one just doesn't talk about this sort of thing in its initial stages. It isn't good business." He paused. "Now, on your side, whom do you think knew?"

"To my certain knowledge, Uncle Simon and Uncle Edgar," Eleanor told him gravely. "And, to my almost certain knowledge, no one else. Because, if he had told anyone else, don't you think, in the circumstances, it would have been me?"

"I think that's a fair assumption." Jervis sat down again, his hands deep in his pockets. "You spoke of a letter—it told you about the idea of a merger? Yes? Well, when was it written? What I'm getting at is this— is it possible that someone had an opportunity of seeing it?"

"No—at least, if they did, it couldn't have been the source of the gossip, because Uncle didn't write it until after I'd been asked by Mother and Geoff if there was anything in it. You can see for yourself." And taking out the letter she had brought in her bag, she handed it to him.

He read it through in silence, referred back to one or two passages and then handed it back to her.

"Yes, that's definite enough," he admitted. His scowl deepened. "So we're just where we were."

"There is another possibility," Eleanor suggested, putting the letter back into her handbag. "Perhaps someone overheard something—possibly, for instance, on the occasion when you dined with Uncle Simon at Kingsworthy."

"When I what?" There was no mistaking his bewilderment. "But I've never dined with your uncle in my life!"

"Oh, come, Mr. Stapleton," Eleanor said impatiently. "You drove your car round to the stables at the back of the house and asked if it would be all right for you to park there. My fiancé, to whom you spoke, confirms that."

"You've got a good grapevine," Jervis remarked drily. "And it's perfectly true. I did ask that—and I believed I even mentioned that I was dining, didn't I?"

"You did!"

"And so I was," Jervis said calmly. "But not with Mr. Simon Chalfont." He looked at her with his head a little on one side as if he was interested in her reaction to what he went on to say. "It was, in fact, with Mrs. Edgar Chalfont and her two children. Her husband was not present."

"What?" Eleanor exclaimed incredulously.

"Perfectly simple, really," Jervis told her. "I was driving back to Kingswell from London and about a mile from your home I saw a girl who was limping badly. I thought I recognised her, and I stopped and asked if I could give her a lift. It was your cousin, Miss Celia Chalfont. She was glad of the lift and I brought her back to the East Pavilion. It was just about dinner time and, I imagine, as an expression of gratitude, I was asked to stay—with rather embarrassing insistence. Rather than make a fuss, I accepted. Mrs. Edgar suggested I should park the car at the back, and though I couldn't see why—"

"Your car is pretty well known—and Uncle Simon's windows overlook the drive in front of the East Pavilion," Eleanor pointed out drily.

"I see. Yes, perhaps that explains it. But whether or not that is the answer, I can assure you that nothing was said on that occasion which could possibly have been taken to refer to this merger business."

"So still we're no nearer," Eleanor replied, though she wasn't really to sure about that. In the back of her mind was an uneasy conviction that of all the members of the Chalfont family, Aunt Alice was the least loyal and discreet. "Not," she went on, standing up, "that it really matters, Mr. Stapleton. You see, there will be no merger!"

To her amazement, Jervis nodded.

"I think you're quite right, Miss Chalfont," he said coolly. "Because, in view of the fact that my father will be retiring at the end of this year, it would mean that you and I had to work together—and I can't see that being a success! Can you?"

"No, I can't," Eleanor said resentfully. "But I can't see why you—"

Jervis laughed with genuine amusement.

"Oh come, Miss Chalfont, you've got your prejudices, you must allow me mine! And mine is that due, no doubt to the fact that there undoubtedly *is* prejudice against women occupying important positions in commerce, they are inclined to be on the defensive all the time. And that makes it very difficult for a woman to differentiate between prejudice against her and a perfectly honest opinion which, however, doesn't line up with her own. Now, I feel very strongly that it is necessary to have complete mutual trust between partners, and that, I'm pretty sure, we would never achieve. Do I make myself clear?"

"Perfectly," Eleanor said coldly. "And now, if you'll be so good as to ring up for a taxi to take me home—"

"Oh, I'll take you—when we've finished our talk together," he told her coolly. "Cigarette?"

"No, thank you—and I would prefer a taxi—"

Completely ignoring her request, Jervis lit himself a cigarette and regarded her thoughtfully for a moment.

"So we're both agreed that a merger is out of the question," he said thoughtfully. "But we haven't yet discussed the question of a take-over—"

"There's nothing to discuss," Eleanor said shortly. "I thought I'd made that perfectly clear."

"Oh, you did," Jervis acknowledged with maddening calm. "But you might have changed your mind."

"I haven't," Eleanor snapped.

"No, you haven't," Jervis said deliberately. "In fact, I'd say that if anything, your mind is still more firmly made up over that than it was before this evening. May I know why?"

Eleanor hesitated. Not by any strength of the imagination could she imagine being on friendly terms with

Jervis. On the other hand, he was not the sort of man one wanted for an enemy.

"Come, let's hear it," he said encouragingly. "You're not afraid to speak your mind, are you?"

"Oh no," Eleanor told him. "Just—I was trying to decide how to say what I feel so that there can be no possible chance of you not understanding. Perhaps it would be best to put it as simply as possible."

"Undoubtedly," Jervis agreed gravely.

"Then—I just don't trust you, Mr. Stapleton. And nothing that has happened this evening has altered my feelings. In fact, as you say, my mind is even more firmly made up than it was before not to have any dealings with you."

"I see. Well, that's clear enough. So we go our own separate ways, regardless of common sense, simply in order to pander to your unreasonable mistrust—"

"Is it so unreasonable?" Eleanor flashed. "Doesn't it occur to you that I've every reason to believe that you have no intention of considering any other interests than your own? How else is it possible to explain the way in which you badgered Uncle Simon so mercilessly over a merger that he had that final heart attack?"

Jervis looked at her a moment without replying.

"You really believe that?" he asked gravely at length.

Eleanor shrugged her shoulders. She had expected a vigorous, even violent rebutment of the suggestion, and this serious consideration of it was disconcerting because it mean that in all fairness she must produce real evidence to support her statement.

"I've no absolute proof that I'm right," she admitted shortly. "But if you remember, in his letter, Uncle Simon made it very clear—"

"That he heartily wished he could shed his responsibilities with the same ease that one takes off a coat," Jervis reminded her sternly. "As he could have done had he been a younger and fitter man, because then the necessarily complicated discussions and decisions wouldn't have bothered him. But he'd left it too late—and he knew and regretted it. The whole tone of his letter makes that perfectly clear."

Eleanor shrugged her shoulders.

"Of course, you can no doubt read just what it suits you to in his letter," she said distantly. "But you seem to have forgotten the final paragraph!"

"That I like my own way and become impatient if I don't get it?" Jervis recalled quietly. "But, if you remember, your uncle admitted to the same fault—if it is a fault."

"Really, it's no good us discussing this any further," Eleanor said impatiently. "We'll never see things from the same point of view, so why waste time over it? If you'll be so good as to ring up for a taxi—"

His lips pressed tightly together, Jervis went out of the room without replying. A few moments later John Vance came in with Eleanor's fur over his arm.

"I'll run you home, if that's agreeable to you," he said cheerfully as he handed the fur to her.

"Thank you," Eleanor said stiffly. Just what, she wondered, had Jervis said to his brother-in-law in explanation for this request to take his place? Just how much did the family know?

That was a question to which she got no answer during the short drive to her home. John talked easily and pleasantly, but only on subjects which couldn't possibly be controversial—the holiday he and Dodie were taking a little later that year while the two children were left with their grandparents, an amusing reference to his hobby which was coin collecting.

"And believe it or not, I've been served up with that old chestnut, a Roman coin dated 55 B.C.! And it took me a long time to convince its owner that it simply must be a fake! Have you any particular hobby, Miss Chalfont?"

Eleanor had to confess that she hadn't, though she was, perhaps, more than usually interested in fans.

"Only there aren't many about now," she explained, "so as a hobby, it hasn't had a chance of developing."

And then John made the one remark which could possibly have been read as referring to her disagreement with Jervis.

"That's a pity," he said, suddenly serious. "For one thing, it's a particularly charming hobby, and well worth considerable effort to indulge it. And for another—in my opinion, everyone ought to have a hobby. That is, if by that you mean something which gives one real pleasure without any consideration of the profit motive. That would absolutely wreck everything because the great thing over a hobby is that it gives one a sort of balance in life. Saves one putting so much of oneself into one's job so that it becomes an obsession—"

There was no need for Eleanor to reply because by then John had stopped outside the West Pavilion and there was no need for her to do any more than thank him for bringing her home as he helped her out.

He lifted his hand in a friendly salute and smiled.

"A pleasure," he assured her, and drove off as Eleanor let herself into the Pavilion.

But later, in her own room, her thoughts turned to what John had said.

A hobby, in his opinion, gave one a sort of balance in life. It prevented work becoming an obsession—

Did that mean that when one's work was one's hobby as well, as was the case both with Uncle Simon and Uncle Edgar, it did make too great a bias in one particular direction—gave too great an importance to something which ought to play only a part in one's life?

It was more or less what Geoff felt, though he had tackled the situation from a different angle. Were they both right? And if so, was it possible for her to save herself from making that particular mistake?

When, a long time later, she did drop off to sleep, the problem was still unsolved in her mind.

*   *   *

Almost immediately, following her visit to the Stapletons' house, life became, by comparison, so tranquil that Eleanor was both grateful and apprehensive. It seemed too good to be true, particularly as she didn't altogether like admitting to some of the causes for such a state of affairs. And the principal item under this heading was undoubtedly that Geoff went off with a string of pupils to join in a pony-trek holiday in Shropshire.

It seemed so disloyal to feel more at ease because Geoff was away, but it was undeniably the truth. Geoff, these days, said little about the way in which Eleanor's free time was so much more restricted, even when, as, more than once, she had to delay or even cancel an outing which they had planned, but that, she knew, didn't mean that he had accepted the situation. It simply was that having put his point of view clearly before her, there was nothing more he could do. It was up to her to decide how she was going to plan her future without constant nagging from him.

Even when she had given him an outline of what had happened about the question of a merger at the Stapleton's he had merely said : "I see," and had neither asked questions nor given an opinion. Nor had either of them referred to the possibility of a complete take-over, Eleanor because she was afraid that if Geoff knew that Jervis would welcome such a development, they might well have a quarrel which it would be impossible to patch up. Geoff presumably didn't mention the idea because she had already convinced him that she would never agree to it.

About the same time that Geoff went off, Kitty, too, left for a holiday. A friend of her stage days, married to an extremely wealthy Greek, suddenly remembered her existence, and invited her to join them on their private yacht for a Mediterranean cruise. Kitty was in ecstasies. Nothing like this had happened to her in years, and she accepted joyfully, though she evidently felt a mild uneasiness on Eleanor's score.

"If only they had asked you as well it would have been quite perfect," she mourned. And then, brightening up : "But look here, darling, why shouldn't I write to Stephanie and ask her if you can come? She's not the sort who would take offence, and that yacht of theirs looks about the size of one of the Queens, judging by the photograph she sent! How about it?"

But Eleanor, knowing that quite apart from her business ties, it just wouldn't be her sort of holiday, and that she might quite likely spoil her mother's spontaneous pleasure if she went, wouldn't hear of it. Kitty was inclined to protest, but Eleanor diverted her by bringing up the question of clothes.

"Because you're sure to need smarter things than you wear here, aren't you?" she suggested.

Kitty agreed that she certainly would and spent a joyous week up in London prior to her holiday restocking her wardrobe. She came back guiltily aware that she had spent far more than she had reckoned to, but was so delighted with all her purchases that even if she had wanted to, Eleanor wouldn't have had the heart to blame her for her extravagance.

"It's ages since you've had any fun, Mother," she said, thinking to herself how absurd it was that Kitty should be half apologising to her. It was the wrong way round—as if she was the older generation and Kitty the younger. Which was, of course, simply because it was Eleanor who would be paying for this near-trousseau.

And, in her heart of hearts, Kitty wondered if it wasn't going to be just that. She had read extracts of Stephanie's letter to Eleanor, but she had not given it to her to read because, in one paragraph, Stephanie had been very frank.

"After all, Kit, you're only forty-three, and that's too young, these days, for a woman to give up! You ought to have some fun—and you ought to find someone to share it with. Now, Greg's got a business friend, an American, who's coming with us on this trip. A bachelor but not, I'd say, a confirmed one. Just the right woman hasn't come his way. And what I say is, why shouldn't you be the right one? Propinquity, moonlit nights, an easy, happy-go-lucky atmosphere—well, there it is. Nothing may come of it, but you never know! And at least you'll have had the fun of the trip!"

No, decidedly, it wasn't for Eleanor to read that! Not that Kitty thought she would really mind having a stepfather, but there was no doubt about it, Stephanie was pretty outspoken, and decidedly Eleanor wouldn't like the idea of her mother deliberately setting out to catch a rich husband. Kitty wasn't sure that she liked it herself, but then, of course, as Stephanie said, nothing might come of it. She and this man, whose name she didn't even know at present, might not take to each other at all. And she certainly had no intention of marrying anyone if she didn't really like them!

So Kitty left with an incredible amount of luggage and Eleanor was alone in the West Pavilion—or had imagined that she would be. But it didn't work out quite like that. Uncle Edgar and Aunt Alice went to Bournemouth and Dick, Celia's twin, went camping in Scotland. Celia would be going off a week later to stay with friends, but in the meantime, Alice Chalfont suggested, in a way that made refusal difficult, that her daughter should stay with Eleanor.

"I don't really like her being alone," she explained to Eleanor. "Oh, I know she's very grown up for her age, but all the same—and you must be lonely, Eleanor—"

Not for the world would Eleanor have confessed that the quiet evenings with no one feeling she was being rather unkind if she didn't talk, were just exactly what she needed. Nor did there seem to be any point in reminding her aunt that after Celia did go away, she, Eleanor, would simply have to put up with being on her own. That was something that wouldn't have appealed to Aunt Alice!

So Celia came over to the West Pavilion and had Kitty's room. She was a tall, slim, pale-faced girl who had never shown any particular signs of wanting to be friendly with Eleanor, but after their first quite pleasant evening together, Eleanor began to wonder if this wasn't because they had never spent any time alone together before. Because there was no doubt about it, one couldn't always behave naturally in front of parents, particularly when, as in Celia's case, one is rather a recessive character and one's mother clearly regards one as a child still—and not a very bright one at that.

But it was not until their third evening together that Celia really unburdened herself. She began diffidently by asking if her mother had said anything to Eleanor about the world trip she wanted Celia to have.

"No, not a word," Eleanor told her with interest. "But then why should she?"

"Because Daddy says it's out of the question," Celia explained. "He says it's far too expensive. So Mummy tackled Uncle Simon about it—that was just a few weeks before he died."

"And was he going to do anything about it?" Eleanor asked quickly, as memory began to stir.

"Not at first," Celia said candidly. "But you know

what Mother is like—she doesn't give up easily. She kept on at him—and she thought Uncle Simon was weakening. She told me that just after the last time she saw him—"

"When was that?" Eleanor asked—and the answer she got did not surprise her in the least.

"The evening before he died."

"I see," Eleanor said quietly. "And you think, now that he's dead, she'll ask me?"

"Sure to," Celia said confidently. "You've got Uncle Simon's money—and you know Mother! But at least it's something that she's held off so far. It gives me a chance to get in first. Eleanor—" she leaned forward, drew a deep breath, and said very earnestly : "Please, *please* if —when she does ask you, say : '*No*' and stick to it, will you?"

"You mean you don't like the idea?" Eleanor said in astonishment. "I should have thought you'd have been frightfully keen about it."

"Well, I'm not," Celia declared bluntly. "And nor would Mummy be if it weren't for the fact that—" she came to an abrupt halt, regarding Eleanor dubiously.

"Look here," Eleanor said reasonably, "I'll be honest with you. I'm not going to pay out a big sum such as would be involved in a trip like this without knowing a lot more about it. And I don't think it's unfair to her to say that your mother will undoubtedly give me her reasons for wanting to pack you off like this—so hadn't you better tell me why you don't want to go? It's probably the only chance you'll have, you know."

"Well, all right," Celia agreed, her eyes falling to her restless hands which were twisting her handkerchief into a knot. "You were right when you said Mother wanted to pack me off. That's exactly it—"

"Yes, but why?" Eleanor asked, and saw the delicate colour rise in Celia's cheeks. "Or shall I guess? There's —someone you're particularly interested in, and for some reason or other Aunt Alice doesn't approve. Is that it?"

"Yes, that's it exactly," Celia said with evident relief, and waited for Eleanor to guess still more.

"You're not very helpful, are you?" Eleanor suggested

good-humouredly. "Well, I suppose the vital question is, why does she object? Is she right to want to give you a chance to get over it—because I suppose that's the idea?"

"Oh yes, that's the idea," Celia agreed. "But it wouldn't make any difference. I love him, and I always shall."

Well, that might or might not be true, but it certainly wasn't a thing to be argued about because it simply couldn't be proved, one way or the other.

"Yes—but try to look at it from your mother's point of view for a moment," Eleanor suggested. "Is there any real reason why she should object? I mean, is he a married man, or has he a bad character in any way—"

"No, of course not," Celia said indignantly. And then, a little less sure of herself, "He's—more or less engaged to another girl, but I don't think it will ever really come to anything—they won't get married, I mean."

"Oh—" Eleanor said uncertainly. "Has he—has he ever said anything to suggest he's in love with you?"

"Good gracious, no," Celia said promptly. And then, seeing Eleanor's obvious perplexity, she went on earnestly: "Look, Eleanor, I know I love him. I think, if it weren't for—the other girl, he might find he loves me. But I may be wrong. And if I am, if he really cares for her enough to marry her, then neither of them will ever know how I feel about him. I've got a bit too much pride for that! But what I am determined about is that I won't be packed off like this! If—if one of these days he finds out he's made a mistake, then I want to be around. That's all."

"You realise that could mean you got rather badly hurt?" Eleanor said gently. "I mean, you may be mistaken—"

"I know. I've said so," Celia said matter-of-factly. "But I think it's a chance worth taking. And after all, it is my life!"

"Yes, it is," Eleanor agreed. "But look here, Celia, if I do turn the idea down, what are you going to do? I mean, you're finished with school now, and I've gathered you aren't interested in going to a university—"

"It's not only that I'm not interested. The university

wouldn't be," Celia explained cheerfully. "I just haven't got that sort of brain. I'd rather do things with my hands."

"What sort of things?" Eleanor asked with interest.

"Well, of course, what I really want to do is get married right away and have at least four babies," Celia said frankly. "But as second best, I'd like to work at our potteries. Not in the office, but learn the practical side from the bottom up. And then specialise in design. But I'd never be allowed to do it. The parents are all against it. I can understand that over Mother, of course. She hates Chalfont's, you know. She sees it as a sort of greedy, grasping monster. But Father—I did think he'd have backed me up. But he didn't. And it wasn't just because of what Mother had said," she added forlornly. "I could tell it was because he didn't want me. I wish I knew why," and she looked at Eleanor questioningly.

"I've no idea," Eleanor told her. "In fact, I didn't know until now that you're interested in the work." She pondered for a moment. "You're really serious about this?"

"I am," Celia said with convincing solemnity.

"Then I'll do what I can about it. But you've got to understand that when members of the same family work together there are—" she hesitated, "stresses and strains which quite likely don't occur when the ties aren't so close. Now, I'm determined that there shall be no increase of those strains if I can help it—"

"And rather than that there should be, you might find you couldn't lend me a hand?" Celia nodded. "Yes, I do understand—and I don't envy you," she added frankly. "I think you've got a rotten job!"

"A difficult one, anyway," Eleanor acknowledged with a sigh. "And now let's forget all about this, shall we, and watch the television. There's what promises to be quite an amusing play coming on almost at once—"

* * *

Postcards—from Geoff saying that the weather was foul, but they were enjoying themselves none the less. From Kitty saying that the weather was marvellous and she was having a wonderful time. And one from Aunt Alice—

Each one ended up: "Love—" and the signature which made Eleanor sigh and smile. What different things "love" could mean!

Aunt Alice and Uncle Edgar were the first to return, and the following evening they entertained Eleanor to dinner as a slight return, so Aunt Alice said, for Eleanor's kindness to Celia.

"And that reminds me," Aunt Alice said blandly. "After dinner, I'd like to have a talk with you about my little girl, Eleanor."

"Of course," Eleanor said, trying not to feel dismayed. It wasn't difficult to guess what the talk was going to be about!

And she was right! It was true that Mrs. Chalfont began a long way off from the real point, but she got there eventually, and when she did, she announced unblushingly that dear Simon had promised to be fairy godmother over giving little Celia this marvellous opportunity of broadening her mind.

"Oh, if only she hadn't said that!" Eleanor thought regretfully. Now there was nothing for it but a head-on collision. "When did Uncle Simon promise that?" she asked gravely.

"When?" Mrs. Chalfont looked disconcerted. "Well, actually it was the night before he collapsed," she admitted reluctantly. "That's why I haven't said anything until now. It didn't seem quite right, somehow, immediately after his death—" She looked hopefully at Eleanor. "Well?"

"Aunt Alice, I think I'd better be quite frank about it," Eleanor said quietly. "I was with Uncle Simon the following morning when you ran through. He asked you if you were intending continuing the conversation you'd had with him the previous night because if so, you were wasting your time because he hadn't changed his mind. So I think you must have misunderstood him—"

Alice Chalfont stood up. Of all the bad luck that she should have chosen that particular moment to ring up and that Eleanor should have been listening!

"Of course, if you like to listen to private conversations and make use of them—" she began offensively.

"It wasn't like that at all, Aunt Alice," Eleanor said wearily. "Uncle could have asked me to go out of his study if he'd wanted to, but he didn't. As for making use of what I heard—"

"Well?" Alice demanded. "Are you going to do anything to help your cousin or not? Because I may as well tell you, there's more to this than just a pleasure or even an educational trip. Celia, foolish child, imagines she is in love—most unsuitably, of course. It always is like that at her age. So I want to give her a chance to get over it—"

"I don't think that's a good enough reason," Eleanor told her gravely. "Celia's grown up, Aunt Alice. Oh yes, she is. Twenty going on for twenty-one is grown up, these days. She's surely got the right to choose whom she'll marry—and in any case, isn't opposition likely to be just the very thing that will make her refuse even to think of changing her mind?"

"I don't want any instructions from you on how to treat my own child," Mrs. Chalfont said, breathing heavily. And then, quite inexplicably to Eleanor, she went on: "This is your last chance, Eleanor! Will you do as I ask or not?"

"Certainly not without discussing it with Celia and giving it a lot more thought than I've had time to do so far," Eleanor said firmly.

"Very well," Mrs. Chalfont said ominously. "But I warn you, you're going to regret this, Eleanor! Regret it with all your heart!"

And shut her thin lips firmly as if, indeed, the last word had been spoken.

CHAPTER VI

THE more Eleanor thought about it, the more convinced she was that now her Uncle Edgar had returned from holiday, the two of them must discuss the present situation in far greater detail than they had done so far, even though he might be reluctant to do so.

It was all very well for him to say that he wasn't a business man, but he was a partner in the firm, even if his interest wasn't as big as her own. And while he had assured her of his loyalty and said that it was for her to make the decisions, as Simon had done, she had known that in turning down the idea of a merger with Stapleton's, she was doing what he had hoped she would. But that he wouldn't have accepted their rivals taking them over, she was quite sure. And if he had felt sufficiently strongly about it, his loyalty might well have wavered, and then where would she have been? Stapleton's wouldn't have been content with even the lion's share. They—which meant Jervis—would have wanted entire control and the whole deal would have been off if Uncle Edgar had refused to sell his interest.

So there simply must be a stronger liaison between Uncle Edgar and herself because, though she had refused to consider selling out to Stapleton's, one had to take a practical and long term view of the future. Changes might well be unavoidable—indeed, they would have to if she was to have any life of her own.

After all, Uncle Edgar, though she might persuade him to take a greater part in the management of the firm, was an elderly man now. Sooner or later he would be dropping out of the firm. He simply must appreciate that and realise that it would be only sensible for her, at the very least, to take someone into partnership.

"I can't—and I won't—accept it that running the firm is my life work," she told herself rebelliously. "And Uncle Edgar will have to accept that! Just as he will have to see that it can't carry on being just Chalfont's. We'll have to have another partner. Of course, there's Richard—but it will be years before he's old enough or knows enough about the work to take over. No, there's *got* to be someone to bridge the gap between Uncle Edgar and Richard—if he wants to come into the firm. Perhaps he doesn't. I've never heard anything to suggest that he does. But then, until she told me herself, I'd no idea that Celia was at all interested. Oh well, I'll just have to wait and see."

In the end, she decided not to approach her uncle immediately since she felt she wanted a little more time to prepare her case, and to think up replies to all the possible objections that her uncle might raise. And within a day or so she was extremely glad she had done so, for an interview with Mr. Franklin brought to her knowledge something whose significance was instantly apparent. She had explained her decision to Mr. Franklin, who nodded thoughtfully but did not answer immediately.

"An excellent idea—if you can put it across," he said drily. "Personally I'm not at all sure that you will be able to—certainly not unless you're very well prepared for every possible argument and obstruction."

"That's why I haven't said anything yet," Eleanor explained eagerly. "I wanted to think things out—"

"Quite so," Mr. Franklin agreed crisply. "But from what you've said, I'm reasonably sure that you are leaving one extremely important fact out of your calculations."

"Am I?" Eleanor asked a little resentfully. "I thought I'd been pretty thorough!"

"So you have. So you have. But the matter to which I am referring was a private arrangement between your two uncles as a result of which Edgar's income from the firm was far nearer to that of Simon than would seem probable."

"Oh?" Eleanor said blankly. "I don't understand."

"No, you wouldn't," Mr. Franklin agreed. "As I said, it was a private arrangement between the two brothers. You know, of course, that your Uncle Edgar has done a lot on the design side?"

"Why, yes, of course."

"What, presumably, you don't know is that, by agreement with Simon, Edgar retained the copyright on those designs," Mr. Franklin went on, speaking with a deliberation which made it clear just how much importance he attached to the information. "Consequently, when his designs were used, he was paid a royalty by the firm, which really meant that *Simon* paid since, where Edgar was concerned, he was simply paying his share of the royalties to himself—taking it from one hand and putting it in the other."

"Yes, I see," Eleanor said abstractedly, realising that this was really the least important detail of what Mr. Franklin had told her. She wrinkled her forehead as she considered the real significance of his statement. "You say that it was a private arrangement, yet you know all about it. Does that mean it was something more than just a verbal agreement?"

"Yes, indeed. It was a legally executed document which I personally drew up. Only one other person in my office saw it—my secretary who typed it and who, I assure you, would no more divulge a client's affairs than I would myself."

"I see," Eleanor said once again, and went on curiously: "I wonder whether Aunt Alice knows about it?"

Mr. Franklin shrugged his shoulders.

"As to that, I wouldn't like to give a definite opinion, but remembering her outburst when she heard the contents of Simon's will, there is certainly a possibility that she doesn't."

"I should think it could be put even more strongly than that," Eleanor said thoughtfully, feeling that here might be the explanation of Aunt Alice's appeal to Uncle Simon for help over sending Celia abroad—and his unequivocal refusal to do anything of the sort. "It seems to me a very strange sort of agreement—one which might have produced all sorts of difficulties and complications if my two uncles had disagreed over anything."

"That I pointed out at the time," Mr. Franklin told her. "But they were both quite sure they knew what they were doing. That I had to accept."

"And am I equally bound by this agreement?" Eleanor asked with considerable concern.

"As regards any designs used by the firm before Simon's death, yes. With regard to any future designs, no—unless, of course, you decide to enter into a similar agreement with Edgar."

"I don't think that's something I can settle in a few minutes," Eleanor said slowly. "I must make sure I really understand just how far I'm committing myself first—"

"I agree entirely," Mr. Franklin said emphatically. And then, thoughtfully : "I came to the conclusion that Simon had agreed to these terms because he had never felt quite happy about the way in which the lion's share of the firm had come to him, under their father's will, while Edgar got so little."

"And yet when it came to a question of making his own will, he did nothing to rectify the injustice," Eleanor said quickly. "Even though he knew this agreement which had evened things up would come to an end with his own death."

"Exactly!" Mr. Franklin replied, closing his briefcase with an emphatic snap.

* * *

Eleanor went home that night—it was a Friday—tired out and feeling completely frustrated. Whichever way she turned she came up against difficulties and obstacles—and this most recent information she had received from Mr. Franklin worried her most of all.

Why hadn't Uncle Simon referred to the agreement in that long and discursive letter of his? And even more disturbing, why hadn't Uncle Edgar spoken of it since? Was he just taking it for granted that she would automatically continue on the same terms? On the face of it, if an experienced man of business as Uncle Simon had been had found it acceptable, then why shouldn't she?

But there was a difference, of course. And it lay in the relationship between two brothers, of whom Edgar had been the younger, and now, an uncle and a niece. And more than ever, to Eleanor's mind, it came to the old problem, if they disagreed, would Edgar be able to accept her decisions with the loyalty he had shown his brother? She just didn't know—and finding out wouldn't be pleasant.

She turned in at the gates of Kingsworthy House with a sense of relief that, for the next two days, she could escape from her problems. Geoff would be arriving home early the following morning and they had planned an outing together. It would be an escape to which she had been looking forward all the week—

But when she reached the West Pavilion, Celia was waiting on the terrace for her. Eleanor, who felt she had grown to know and understand her young cousin better than she had ever done before since they had spent those few weeks together, waved a greeting—but met with no response.

"What is it?" Eleanor asked apprehensively, her own smile fading.

"Geoff's had an accident," Celia blurted out.

Eleanor felt the colour drain from her face, and the hand she laid on Celia's arm was shaking.

"Tell me," she demanded sharply.

"Well, he tried to get you on the phone and then as he didn't get a reply—" Celia began when Eleanor interrupted her.

"You mean he's not badly hurt?" she said quickly, "He couldn't have been if he rang up himself—" She swallowed convulsively. "Celia, you might have been a bit more thoughtful—just what has happened?"

"Well, he couldn't get you, so he rang through to us," Celia said rather sulkily. "He's wrenched his knee—his horse was startled by a traction engine and threw him."

"Oh, poor Geoff!" Eleanor said, genuinely concerned yet on the whole relieved. "How absolutely rotten for him! So what's he doing?"

"He's booked in at a small local hotel for a few days to give it a rest," Celia explained, a growing note of resentment in her voice. "He gave me the address, but he said don't phone because he'd have to go downstairs to answer it and it would be just asking for trouble."

"Yes, of course," Eleanor said, her heart sinking. So, after all, she wouldn't be able to escape with Geoff for a few hours tomorrow! It really was the last straw!

"Well?" Celia demanded fiercely. "What are you going to do about it?"

For a moment Eleanor thought her cousin had somehow been able to read her thoughts. Then she realised that it was something quite different which was concerning her. She was looking at it entirely from Geoff's point of view, and that, Eleanor told herself a little guiltily, was what she ought to have done. And yet—

"There isn't much I can do since he doesn't want to telephone, is there?" she pointed out. "I shall write, of course."

"You'll write, of course!" Celia repeated mockingly. "And he'll get it on Monday—that means two whole days stuck there with nobody to talk to and nothing to do—you make me furious, Eleanor!"

Eleanor stared at her blankly.

"What on earth are you talking about, Celia?" she asked, exasperated at being taken to task for, as far as she could see, no reason at all. "Of course it will be dull for Geoff, not to mention the fact that he'll probably be in pain. But Geoff isn't a child, you know. He—well, he'll just put up with it because he isn't the sort to make a fuss."

"No, he isn't, more's the pity," Celia agreed. "It would be better for him and everybody else if he was."

"And just what does that mean?" Eleanor asked quietly, reluctant to discuss her and Geoff's most private affairs and yet feeling that it was probably better that she should be the one to hear the outburst which was obviously coming than that anyone else should.

"Just what I said," Celia declared truculently. "Geoff's the sort of person who is very easily hurt, and if he has to fight for himself—for things that ought to be given to him—then it spoils everything. Oh, do stop looking so surprised! You ought to know it for yourself!"

Eleanor did know it. In different words Geoff had said much the same thing. What surprised her was that Celia knew it as well.

"I don't suppose it's the least bit of good telling you to mind your own business because you so obviously feel that it *is* yours," she said, hoping that the slight edge to her voice would make at least some impression on Celia. "So you'd better get it off your chest! Just what do you think I ought to do? Or, put it another way, if you were me, what would you do?"

For a moment Celia was too taken aback at this permission to speak her mind to take advantage of it. Then, stammering in her eager earnestness, the flood was let loose.

"What would I do? What would I do? Well, for one thing, I wouldn't be engaged to a man unless I loved him with all my heart and soul! And feeling like that, if—if anything happened to him as it has done to Geoff, I'd—I'd go to him even if it was to the ends of the earth instead of perhaps a hundred miles or so. That's what *I'd* do!"

And it was what Eleanor would have done, not so very long ago. But now, no, not when there was this barrier of different viewpoints between them. If Geoff had asked her to go, even just hinted, it might have been different. Perhaps, had she taken his call, he might have done—

"Did Geoff ask you to say this to me?" she asked on an impulse, and saw Celia's eyes drop.

"No, he didn't," she confessed reluctantly. "And you ought to know he wouldn't," she added with another sudden burst of confidence. "He's too proud to do a thing like that!"

"Pride?" Eleanor repeated almost to herself. "Does that come into it?"

"Of course it does," Celia declared scornfully. "Look, ever since you and he got engaged we all understood that you were going to be married this August. Right?"

"Yes," Eleanor breathed the word on a sigh.

"All right. Well now, we're part way through July and you don't appear to be making any more definite plans than you did eighteen months ago! No signs of any invitations being sent out, nothing done about your wedding dress—and your mother still away with apparently no intention of coming back yet! Does that sound like a wedding in August? I don't think it does—and nor does Geoff, I'm quite sure! So is it likely, seeing you're so evidently enjoying being the big business executrix so much, that he'd risk another snub after the one you've given him already?"

"All right, Celia, you've said enough—more than enough," Eleanor, white to the lips, spoke very quietly. "You've told me what you think. Well, there are other points of view—"

"Other points of view!" Celia interrupted passionately. "There's only one other—yours! You were quite pleased to be going to marry Geoff before Uncle Simon left you all his money, but now Geoff isn't good enough for you, is he? You're rich and he's poor—a man who prefers to do the job he really loves rather than just make money! Well, I know what I think! You're not good enough for him! He deserves absolutely the best—"

Her voice trailed away as she saw something in Eleanor's eyes—an understanding that made her turn tail and rush back to the far end of the house.

Eleanor stood in frozen stillness until the slamming of the East Pavilion door startled her to movement. She took her key out of her handbag and then, impulsively, pushed it back into her bag and got back into her car.

Four walls and a roof would stifle her. She must get out somewhere where she could breathe freely of air that wasn't charged with emotion—

For quite suddenly she had known Celia's secret. She was in love with Geoff. Everything pointed that way. Celia's own earlier admission that she was in love with a man who was "more or less" engaged to another girl. Her hope that Geoff would one day find out his mistake.

Aunt Alice's insistence that if she didn't pay for Celia to have a long holiday abroad, she herself would be the one to regret it.

Yes, Celia was in love with Geoff. No doubt about that. But Geoff? Was he beginning to feel he had made a mistake?

Her foot came down on the accelerator and she made for the hills. But she was not to make her escape without hindrance.

The route she took necessitated passing Helen Chalfont's little house, and by ill luck, her aunt was out in the road clipping back her hedge. Clearly she expected Eleanor to stop, and because it seemed easier to do so than explain afterwards why she hadn't, she pulled up.

"Hallo, child, I haven't seen much of you lately," Miss Chalfont said, giving Eleanor one of those quick, penetrating looks that made one feel like an open book.

"I've been busy," Eleanor said briskly. "And if you'll

forgive me for being so frank, this is the first time for quite a long while that I've managed to get off on my own and—I'd rather not—" she halted abruptly, her nerves taut to breaking point yet reluctant to hurt her aunt's feelings.

"My dear girl, don't apologise," Helen Chalfont said briskly. "I've too much of the cat that walks alone in me not to know that there are times—off you go! No, wait a minute. I promise it won't be longer and that you won't regret it."

And without waiting for Eleanor to reply, she hurried into the house to return almost immediately with a basket in which was a bottle of milk and two paper bags.

"When you've worked out what you're going to do over—this and that, you'll find you're hungry," she said. "These supplies will mean you don't have to go home just because of that before you really want to!"

"That's marvellous of you," Eleanor said with genuine gratitude. "I want to stay out as long as I possibly can—"

"I thought you might," Helen said casually, turned her back on Eleanor and began to get on with her clipping. She had done her best to show her niece that while she was very willing to do what she could to help, she had no intention of intruding in any way into her private affairs. She hoped the child understood. It was always so difficult to know for sure what other people really thought and felt—most difficult of all when a generation separated the people concerned.

Eleanor had appreciated her aunt's tact, even more than her practical common sense, but none the less she gave little thought to it. Hardly realising the direction she was driving in, she made for Windmill Hill, the one to which Geoff had driven her on the day of Uncle Simon's funeral. Now, as then, the view was superb, but beyond a realisation of the spaciousness and quiet for which she had so longed for, Eleanor was barely conscious of her surroundings, though after a while she realised that they weren't going to be of any help at all to her. The confusion of her mind went too deep for that. And she was very tired. More tired than she had ever been in her life before—

She made a desperate effort to force her brain to activity, but her thoughts blurred into meaningless words and phrases which had nothing whatever to do with her problems, or indeed with anything else.

"No one in their senses *ever* buys burnt bristles," she told someone severely and coming back to reality, heard the echo of the absurd statement, laughed at it, and as quickly forgot all about it to drowse off again.

It was warm and sheltered and very quiet in the little hollow of the hill where she had settled herself. She relaxed more comfortably and slept deeply.

When she woke up, the sun was still warm, but it was lower and she was conscious of a sense of time having passed. For a few moments she lay there luxuriating in the knowledge that there was no need for her to get up in a hurry. For once, her time was her own. But Aunt Helen had been right—or partially right. She hadn't solved her problems, but she was hungry!

She was just about to scramble to her feet when she became aware of a distinctive smell in the air—one that was completely out of place here. The fragrant smoke of a wood fire. Alarmed lest the short, dry grass should have caught fire and, perhaps, she was in some danger, she jumped up, and letting her sense of smell lead her, soon found out what it was all about.

From another hollow, similar to the one she had found, rose a thin wisp of blue smoke emanating from a small fire which was being carefully tended by a man who was squatting with his back to her.

But Eleanor did not need to see his face to know who it was. Of all people, Jervis Stapleton! She must have caught her breath or made some other small sound, for he turned his head and then stood up.

"Hallo, had a good snooze?" he asked as completely at his ease as if they were old friends on the very best of terms.

"Thank you, yes," Eleanor said coldly, annoyed that he had evidently intention of making her feel at a disadvantage.

But he misread the cause of her annoyance—or else pretended to do so.

"I say, I do hope I didn't disturb you," he said with

every appearance of concern. "I had no idea you were here, of course, until I'd almost topped the rise, and though I tried to keep quiet then, I'd made quite a noise crashing up the slope."

It was on the tip of Eleanor's tongue to tell him that he ought to have realised that she had come here in search of solitude, and that if he had had any consideration at all, he would simply have gone on with his walk leaving her in ignorance that he had even passed that way. But to have said that would have laid her wide open to the retort that this was common land, and as such, as much his property as hers.

It might have been that he guessed what was in her mind, for he remarked casually:

"I always come here if I've got anything on my mind," and he made a sweeping gesture with his hand as if to indicate the reason why.

Eleanor was startled into blurting out exactly what the remark had made her think.

"But you are always so sure of yourself! What sort of problems can you possibly have?"

His mouth twitched as if her outspokenness had amused him, but his reply, although it had a specious air of answering with equal frankness, was actually entirely uninformative.

"Oh, the usual sort—the same sort that most of us have. Those caused by things—and people. Particularly people!"

Things and people! Yes, of course, that was absolutely true. But whereas he, she was sure, would always find his own way out of his difficulties, she was feeling with increasing conviction, that without help, she never would.

And then an astonishing thing happened. Utterly out of the blue came a passionate longing to tell this man everything that was troubling her—to surrender to his strength and let him make her decisions for her—

As quickly as the idea had come she dismissed it as impossible, but evidently enough time had passed for him to have said something which she had not heard for he was looking at her enquiringly as if he expected an answer.

"I'm sorry," she had to confess, "I didn't hear what you said—"

"I merely remarked that whenever I come here I light a fire. A picnic doesn't seem complete without one, even if it doesn't play any practical part in proceedings."

"A picnic?" For the first time she noticed that lying at his feet was a small satchel full of knobbly packages.

"Only bread and cheese and lager," Jervis said apologetically, "but I'd be delighted if you'd share it—there is plenty."

Afterwards, it surprised Eleanor to remember that she had not even considered refusing the invitation. She told herself that it had simply been because she was so hungry, but never quite convinced herself that was the true reason.

"I'd like to," she said gravely. "If you'll allow me to contribute to the feast—I've got a basket in my car—"

They spread the meal on a flat outcrop of stone and tucked in with the fervour and steady application of two people very much their junior. Nor did they waste much time talking until suddenly Eleanor exclaimed:

"Do you know, I realise I haven't had a really good meal for weeks!"

Instantly she had said the words she regretted them, but Jervis made no attempt to connect them with what he knew of her circumstances.

"I was in much the same state," he confessed. "I've recently been over to America, and travelling by air, one gets in such a muddle over time that meals seem to be served every hour or so. And then, when I got there, I was greeted with such generous hospitality that all my clothes felt too tight. So when I got back, I rationed myself severely for a week to put things right. Now I must surely have put on weight again, but your sausage rolls were too tempting to resist!"

"They weren't mine," Eleanor explained honestly. "At least, not in the sense of having made them. Aunt Helen did that. She's a marvellous cook."

"Miss Chalfont?" he raised his eyebrows. "Do you mean to say that as well as being a very successful literary lady, she's a good cook?"

"Why not?" Eleanor said with a hint of belligerence.

"Most women can do at least two jobs really well."

But once again Jervis did not accept the challenge she had thrown down. Instead, much to her surprise, he asked :

"Did you know that there was a time when Miss Chalfont might have been *my* aunt as well as yours?"

"Yours?" Eleanor repeated. "I don't understand."

"No? I'll explain. She and my Uncle Lucas—Father's younger brother—met and fell in love. They planned to get married without more ado, but there was opposition from both sides, and Miss Chalfont was very young and inexperienced at the time. She listened to all the nonsense she was told about her family's anxiety for her— she was so young, Mr. Stapleton was no doubt very charming, but she didn't really know him, did she? And so, in the end, she agreed to wait a year to make sure of her feelings—yes? You said something?"

"No," Eleanor assured him hurriedly. "Nothing! Do go on. I've never heard anything about this before—"

"You wouldn't, least of all from Miss Chalfont. Poor soul, she's been regretting that decision ever since. And that means over thirty years, because this happened just before the war. Lucas was a Territorial and was called up immediately. They did decide then that in such circumstances her promise to her parents wasn't binding, but before they could arrange to get married or he could get leave, he was killed."

"Oh, poor Aunt Helen," Eleanor breathed. "All these years—" And what made it all the worse was that history was almost repeating itself. Uncle Simon had said he wanted her to wait a year. But that, of course, had been for a different reason—

"What is so iniquitous is that the real reason why they wanted to stop the marriage had nothing to do with the happiness of the two people concerned. It was purely the outcome of busines rivalry and the determination of both fathers not to surrender an atom of their individuality as they feared might be the case if there was a blood tie between the two families."

"You—you can't be sure of that," Eleanor protested.

"If you mean I can only know of this second hand, that's perfectly true," Jervis agreed. "But I'm quoting my father who was very nearly thrown out along with Lucas for sticking up for him. He's always hated this vicious rivalry. Fair competition, yes. Why not? But when it gets to the degree of hatred—" he shook his head and fell silent.

Vicious rivalry? Hatred? But he surely didn't think that was a fair description of the way things were now? Why, Uncle Simon had seriously considered a merger and she herself—her thoughts came to an abrupt halt. An emotion even stronger than anything business rivalry could have caused had surged up in her that night when she had dined at his home. Something more personal, something that held fear in it—

She realised that Jervis's dark eyes were fixed gravely on her face, and to break the silence she said the first thing that came into her head.

"What I don't understand is how they ever came to meet at all—and how they had a *chance* to fall in love."

"They met, by pure coincidence, week-ending at the house of a common friend," Jervis explained. "Miss Chalfont and the daughter had been at school together. Uncle Lucas and the son had met in Switzerland the year before. As simple as that. And as for a chance to fall in love—well, they had the whole of the weekend! Enough for anybody, surely!"

"Oh!" Eleanor said breathlessly. "Do you really think so?"

"You mean you agree with the parents?" he asked bluntly. "You think they were right to forbid the banns?"

"No, I don't," Eleanor denied stoutly. "But all the same, it *was* quick, wasn't it?"

Jervis shrugged.

"Quick or slow, is that really the most important thing?" he asked seriously. "Judging by what I've seen, people can be both right or wrong in either case. What really matters is—*knowing*. Knowing beyond all possible doubt that here is someone who is more important to you than you yourself are. Recognising something in another person that is—vital to you. Or am I talking a lot of rot? You ought to know. You're the one that's engaged."

"No, you're not talking rot," Eleanor said rather shakily. "I quite agree, for some people, it can happen in a flash. For others—for me—it grew from friendship. Geoff and I have known each other most of our lives—"

"And do you agree with me that either way, people can make mistakes?" he pursued relentlessly.

"Oh, I should think more than likely," she replied, deliberately cool. "Though I can assure you that isn't so in my case!"

"But am I so sure of that?" she wondered silently. *"For myself, yes. But Geoff—"*

"I see," Jervis said thoughtfully. "A pity, that!"

"I beg your pardon?" Eleanor said incredulously.

"A great pity," he told her grimly. And as she continued to stare blankly at him he went on impatiently: "Do you mean to say it hasn't occurred to you that your troubles—and for that matter, mine as well—would dissolve in thin air if—we were to get married?"

CHAPTER VII

ELEANOR stared blankly at Jervis. He simply couldn't have said that! But he had!

"Your troubles—and mine—would dissolve into thin air—if we were to get married!"

How dared he—how *dared* he! She never remembered being so angry in all her life, and knew in her heart that at least some of her anger was due to the fact that, such a short time ago, she had experienced that absurd desire to turn all her problems and perplexities over to him. Surely he hadn't guessed—no, of course he couldn't have done. But she must see to it that she gave him no opportunity of doing so.

But she had little time to think, for he was clearly waiting for an answer. Inspiration came suddenly. Not anger, appallingly bad form though his remark had been. Amusement—that was much better! It might even put him in his place as anger would never do. So she laughed softly.

"Really, Mr. Stapleton, what an odd sense of humour you've got!"

"Humour?" He surveyed her in bland wonder. "But I'm not joking. I meant it quite seriously."

"You did?" Eleanor laughed again and shook her head. "I really can't believe that—and I think you should be glad I can't," she added significantly.

"You mean you do regard marriage as a subject for joking?" he suggested softly.

"Of course I don't," Eleanor retorted crisply. "But in the circumstances, I do find it less offensive to regard what you said as the outcome of a mistaken sense of humour rather than a serious suggestion."

"But I assure you, I had no intention whatever of being offensive," Jervis insisted mildly. "What I said was true. Were we to be married, it would solve many problems. For instance, one about which you already know—the question of us both loosing markets because neither of us does a complete range of qualities and resulting prices. If we were married, our interests would be so identical that we would soon settle that matter. And then, with your profits dropping—"

"Who told you they were?" Eleanor demanded sharply. "Who's been putting such a story about?"

"I could tell you who actually told me," Jervis replied seriously. "And that person told me who his informant was. But to be quite frank with you, though I went to considerable pains to follow the thread, I had no success. All I can say with any certainty is that it appeared to be common knowledge."

"Just as the idea of a merger was," Eleanor mused. "I don't like this, Mr. Stapleton. It means that someone, somewhere, is trying to undermine our credit."

"That's how I read it," Jervis agreed. "Any idea who it might be?"

"No. Have you?" she countered.

"Not really. Sometimes I feel I'm on the brink of— well, let's say, of guessing. No more than that. Then even that fades." He frowned and shook his head. "No, it's all so vague. But at least there's one thing I'm sure of. If we were married, this sort of thing would stop because it would be pointless."

"But what *is* the point of it all?" Eleanor asked impatiently. "Is there one at all?"

"Oh, indeed, yes! Someone—unspecified—wanted to make us think you weren't worth taking over," Jervis explained matter-of-factly.

"Or else someone—again unspecified—hoped that by putting a tale like that about, they might so damage our reputation that they might buy us up more cheaply," Eleanor retorted sharply.

"Yes, there's that possibility as well. And out of all that one can be pretty sure of one very unpleasant fact. The way things are, it's unlikely that the old rivalry between our firms will ever diminish, because, what with one thing and another, it's pretty well impossible for either of us to trust the other. Has someone foreseen that as well, do you think?"

"Oh, I don't know!" Eleanor said desperately. "It's all so complex, and so beastly—"

"And none of it would have happened if we were married or likely to be," Jervis insisted grimly.

"Perhaps you're right," Eleanor sighed hopelessly. "But even if I was not engaged—and you do seem to make rather light of that—of course it wouldn't be possible—"

"No? Why not?" he wanted to know coolly.

"Oh—" Eleanor exclaimed impatiently. "Do I have to spell it out in words of one syllable? Two people just don't get married in order to solve business problems. Is that clear enough?"

"Oh, quite. But you're not telling me anything I didn't know," Jervis told her. "What I meant, of course, is—what a pity it is we haven't fallen in love. Because, if we had, everything would be so simple!"

"Would it?" Eleanor asked ironically, refusing to listen to the quickening of her heart. "A very similar situation didn't have that effect in an earlier generation, did it? Isn't it fair to say that it caused even more trouble? Then why should there be any difference now?"

"Because, if I were certain that I loved a girl and she loved me, I'd handle things differently from the way in which Uncle Lucas did," Jervis explained. "He was wrong to listen to your aunt because he must have known that she was being taken for a ride by her family. He should have protected her from her own simplicity and sweetness."

"How?" Eleanor asked sceptically. "If he'd made her do something she thought was wrong, how could she ever have been really happy with him? And anyhow, what could he have done?"

For a moment or two Jervis regarded her thoughtfully with oddly veiled eyes. Then, very deliberately, he said :

"One can never say with absolute certainty what someone else would have done, but I know what I'd have done in the same circumstances. I'd have taken her into my arms, held on tight, and kissed her until she stopped talking nonsense and got her priorities right—"

"And if that didn't work?" Eleanor asked.

"Oh, then—well, I'd have had to do the modern equivalent of throwing her across my saddle bow and bolting with her to my impregnable castle," Jervis said calmly. "In other words, have a special licence all ready in my pocket and choose just the right time to persuade her to help me make use of it."

"Oh dear, what an anti-climax!" Eleanor protested lightly. "Not nearly so romantic as your first idea. You disappoint me, Mr. Stapleton!"

"Do I? I'm sorry. But you must remember, I'm only giving you a very bare outline plan. There would doubtless be opportunities for improvements here and there. Perhaps you can suggest some?"

Eleanor shook her head. The conversation had gone quite far enough in her opinion. It could become embarrassing unless she put a stop to it now.

"I'm afraid I haven't that sort of imagination. And in any case, what a waste of time! After all, it's purely a hypothetical situation, isn't it? So why bother?"

"Why indeed?" Jervis agreed placidly. "Except that it provides a good example of a discovery I made some time ago."

"Oh?" Eleanor's polite indifference should have discouraged Jervis, but, as she had already discovered, he wasn't the easily discouraged sort. He wasn't now.

"Yes," he explained abstractedly. "It was this—though it may seem an alarmingly drastic course to take, there are times when cutting the Gordian Knot *is* the only way out of an *impasse*. And the simplest and the best."

Eleanor looked at him sharply. Was he just speaking in general terms, or was he implying that she should take the hint to her heart? But he was concentrating all his attention on stamping out the little fire he had kindled and there was nothing in his face to give her an answer, one way or the other.

*   *   *

There was a letter from her mother waiting for Eleanor when she reached home. But when she picked it up off the mat, apart from noticing in a preoccupied way that it bore a Greek stamp, she gave it no further attention.

Whether he had intended to do so or not, Jervis had given her something to think about.

"... *times when cutting the Gordian knot is the only way out of an impasse*—"

Well, of course, that was as true today as when, centuries ago, Alexander had refused to fiddle about with a difficult knot, and had slashed impatiently through it with his sword.

There were times when, in order to achieve anything at all, one had to take the bold line, seeing only one's goal, and refusing to be deflected from it by less important considerations.

That she had already appreciated, but now Jervis had pinpointed the necessity for deciding just what her goal was.

As if there could be any doubt about that! To marry Geoff, of course—not at some vague and distant time in the future. *Now*, just as they planned to do. And nothing and nobody was going to stop that happening.

The more she thought about it, the more right she felt she was, and if she needed any further conviction, she had it in recalling what Geoff himself had said:

"If we once postpone our wedding, we'll never get married!"

THE HEAD OF THE HOUSE

Her heart chilled. At the time, she had thought he was making too much of it. Now she wasn't so sure. It was as if a net, invisible, perhaps, but very strong, was tightening around her.

Had Uncle Simon hoped that delay would mean she didn't get married at all? She could only guess the answer to that. But what she did know was that for both the Chalfont brothers, priorities were totally different from her own. They put their work first, she believed that personal happiness, in this case hers and Geoff's, was more important. Perhaps the difference in outlook was inevitable. She was a woman, they were men. What was more, one had never experienced the deep, warm tie of happy married life. Perhaps neither of them had, for certainly Uncle Edgar was married to a woman who must be very difficult to live with!

Yes, she could see the reason for their point of view, but that didn't mean that it could or should be her own.

She made up her mind what she would do. She would go and see Geoff tomorrow, for after all, as Celia had said, he was only about a hundred miles away. And as for that absurd feeling of hers that there was a barrier between them—well, if there was any truth in that, it was her fault, and it was no wonder that Geoff hadn't suggested that she should pay him a visit. He *would* be too afraid that he would be courting a snub, just as Celia had said.

There was only one thing to decide—should she ring through to the hotel where he was staying to ask them to let him know she was coming? It would be sensible, perhaps, but she wanted to surprise him. She wanted to see the expression on his face when he first saw her.

And she would take a small suitcase with her in the hope that the hotel might have a vacant room.

She would go to bed early and set the alarm to go off at six o'clock. Then she could be on her way by seven, and even if she couldn't find accommodation, at least they could have a long day together.

She made herself a nightcap of a cup of tea and by half-past nine was in bed, to sleep more deeply and tranquilly than she had done for weeks.

*   *   *

When Eleanor started off the following morning there was every promise of it being a fine day. Already the lacy overnight mist was dissolving and the sun glinted diamond-like on the dewy hedges and grass. It was enough to make anyone's spirits rise, particularly when, as in Eleanor's case, she was quite sure that the future was bright with promise. She and Geoff would talk everything over and there would be no more shadows between them.

She was able to take comparatively minor roads on which there was little traffic so early in the morning. In fact, she was only really conscious of one car which kept steadily ahead of her—a small red Mini whose number was just too far off for her to be able to read. For some reason she found its persistent presence vaguely disturbing, and more than once put on speed in the hope of overtaking it—but without success. Whoever was driving it knew their job, and in the end she dropped back a little rather than be irritated in this stupid way.

None the less, she made reasonably good time and finally reached her destination a full half hour before she had expected to. Then she lost a little time hunting for the hotel. Ayebury was not a very big town. Indeed, it was little more than a slightly overgrown village. But the little hotel was tucked away in a side street and it required careful manoeuvring to get past parked cars and into the hotel park.

Not really to her surprise, she found that the red Mini was already parked there—at least, it looked like the same one to her although, of course, it was a very popular model, and in any case, it really wasn't of any importance.

She went into the little hotel and rang the bell at the reception desk. A pleasant-faced woman came through from the office at the rear in reply, and Eleanor made her request. To her satisfaction, there was a spare room, and Eleanor reserved it for the night. Then, when she had signed the register, she enquired after Geoff's whereabouts.

To her surprise, the woman did not reply immediately. Indeed, she looked rather curiously at Eleanor, who, flushing slightly, imagined that the propriety of her coming here so obviously because Geoff was already here was being questioned.

Casually she laid her left hand on the top of the desk, smiled expectantly, and waited silently for an answer. The woman seemed to pull herself together.

"Yes, of course, miss," she said hurriedly. "I'll send one of the maids up to tell him you're here—"

But she didn't move, and Eleanor saw that her eyes were lifted to look at the stairs on the other side of the hall. Eleanor turned, and saw Geoff, leaning on a walking stick, and coming down slowly and awkwardly, his other hand on the banister rail.

And behind him was—Celia.

Celia, who had a red Mini car, and who could only have arrived a few minutes previously—no wonder the receptionist had been puzzled!

Eleanor wished with all her heart that the ground could open and swallow her up, but since that wasn't possible, she knew that it was up to her to make as little of a situation made all the more difficult because the receptionist would hear everything that was said. However—

She strolled over to the foot of the stairs, forced back a rising tide of something very much like panic and said gaily:

"Hallo, Geoff darling!"

She ought to have realised, perhaps, that he would be startled by her unexpected presence, but surely not to the degree of stumbling to an abrupt halt and regarding her open-mouthed with no sign whatever of welcome on his face. For one horrible, fleeting moment, indeed, she even wasn't sure that he didn't look guilty.

Celia had, perforce, also come to a halt, and now she blurted out accusingly:

"You didn't say you were coming!"

It was on the tip of Eleanor's tongue to say:

"Nor did you!"

But obviously that would be unwise, so she substituted a casual:

"I wasn't sure that I could manage it," and went on just as casually: "Were you going to have a drink? I'll join you when I've taken my case up to my room," and turned smilingly to the waiting receptionist. A chambermaid was summoned and Eleanor was just going to follow her upstairs when Geoff, now in the hall, said gruffly:

"We were going to have a drink in the garden."

"Lovely!" Eleanor agreed. "As I came in I thought how attractive it looked, sloping down to the little river! Be with you in a few minutes!"

She ran upstairs, gained the sanctuary of a pleasant little room and, as soon as the maid had gone, sank down exhaustedly on the edge of the bed.

What a situation! Of course, there was no real reason why Celia shouldn't come and see Geoff, but in view of her outburst, Eleanor could hardly fail to wonder whether she intended to keep to her determination not to interfere between the man she loved and the girl he was "more or less engaged to", as she had put it. Of course, she had also said that she wanted to be around if "he" ever found he'd made a mistake. Now, to put it mildly, if, as Eleanor was now perfectly sure, Geoff was the man in question, she was surely going considerably beyond that neutral attitude! Clearly what she had intended to do was to suggest to him, though not perhaps in words, that his fiancée couldn't be bothered to come and see him, but she, Celia, had been only too glad to.

And Geoff, no doubt, had been glad to see her. Why not? It must be very boring for him to be stuck here with no one he knew to talk to, but after all, not only did he know Celia very well, but sooner or later they would be cousins by marriage.

No, as far as Geoff was concerned there was nothing to worry about—at least, not unless Celia had given herself away—that might have happened, and it would explain that odd look on Geoff's face. He must have felt not only embarrassed, but also more than a little apprehensive lest anyone, and in particular Eleanor herself, should think he had encouraged Celia.

She sighed and went over to the dressing table, ran a comb through her hair and mended her make-up. Then, just for a moment, she paused. She couldn't go down to them looking like that—with troubled eyes and a mouth that didn't smile. She curved her lips deliberately, tried to think a sparkle into her eyes—and sighed again. Worse than ever, for it made her look amused. And that Celia would hate even more than if she met with anger. Still, she had got to go down.

She found them sitting on opposite sides of a small rustic table, and it didn't need much intelligence to know that neither of them had found much to say to the other. Geoff looked vexed and ill at ease. Celia, paler even than usual, looked on the point of bursting into tears. Eleanor felt a quick compassion for her. And yet what could she possibly do to comfort this young cousin of hers? Tell her she would get over it? People did sometimes—but they never liked to believe it possible. Agree, after all, to Aunt Alice's request to pay for Celia to have a long, interesting tour of the world? But Celia wouldn't go—

A waiter brought out a tray of drinks and the feeling of tension lessened a little. Eleanor set herself to making conversation, and to her relief, Geoff backed her up. Both of them did their best to draw Celia into the conversation, but without much success. She would answer a direct question, but as briefly as possible, and made no contribution herself at all. She was obviously wishing herself anywhere else but where she was, as her fidgeting hands and the occasional uneasy looks she darted at first one and then the other of them made clear.

But even this was not half so awkward as when, just before lunch, Eleanor felt compelled to ask Celia to use her room to tidy up in. They were no sooner in the room than Celia turned on her.

"I suppose you want to know why I'm here," she asked defiantly.

"I think I can guess." Eleanor was surprised that she could speak so calmly, with such a feeling of being in control of the situation. "You felt sorry for Geoff, and you thought you'd try to cheer him up."

Celia looked at her in a startled, puzzled way.

"And you don't mind?"

"Is there any reason why I should?" Eleanor asked, hoping that the direct question would jolt Celia into seeing that the less she said the better. And for a moment, she thought she had been successful.

"No—" Celia said slowly. And then, recklessly: "Yes, there is. You know there is! Geoff is the man that I—"

"No!" Eleanor interrupted firmly. "I'm not going to listen, Celia! I think you're on the brink of saying something that you'll regret speaking of one of these days. So leave it at that. And please understand, this is something between you and me. No one else. Least of all Geoff. Do you agree?"

"Yes," Celia said in a subdued voice. "I—I don't want to make trouble, honestly I don't, Eleanor. But I thought you didn't care enough to come—"

"And you were mistaken," Eleanor said lightly. "Now, hurry up, or Geoff will be wondering—"

Lunch wasn't a very easy meal to get through, although Celia did her best to talk naturally, and Eleanor did her best to second her. But now it was Geoff who was silent and abstracted. Had he, Eleanor wondered, an inkling of the real reason why Celia had come to see him? Celia, she thought, was wondering the same thing, an idea which was confirmed when, as soon as they had finished their coffee, Celia said that she must go.

"I always prepare the evening meal on Saturdays, so that Mother has a break," she explained rather lamely, and a few minutes later she drove the red Mini out of the car park.

As the sound of the motor died away, Eleanor gave an involuntary sigh of relief, and noticed that Geoff sighed as well. She looked at him quickly and saw something in his face that she had never seen there before— anxiety—a grim determination.

Catching her eyes, he nodded in the direction of her car.

"Are you too tired of driving to go for a short run?" he asked abruptly. "I'd like to have a talk with you somewhere private."

"All right," Eleanor agreed, half relieved, half apprehensive. "But you'll have to tell me where. I've never been in this district before."

She unlocked the car and Geoff got rather awkwardly

into the passenger seat. He gave her brief, simple directions, and in about a quarter of an hour's time they parked in the shelter of a ruined castle, gaunt and forbidding even in the summer sunshine. Shivering a little, Eleanor found a spot in the sunshine and the two of them sat down on a piece of fallen masonry.

For a moment neither of them spoke, then, abruptly, Geoff said :

"Eleanor, I want to go ahead with our original plan to be married in August. Will you?"

She gave a little cry, blended of surprise and relief.

"Why, Geoff, it was to suggest we should that I came to see you!" she exclaimed.

"Was it?" It was his turn to look surprised. "But I thought you'd made up your mind that we ought to wait for at least a few months."

"So I had," she admitted.

"Then what's made you change your mind?"

"Realising that I think you were right," she said soberly. "You said you thought Uncle Simon was banking on the probability that if we once postponed our wedding, we'd never get married."

"I still think that," Geoff said doggedly.

Eleanor nodded.

"I've said I think you were right. But there's something else, Geoff. I don't think it's just what Uncle Simon said in his letter that's making me feel as if—things—people—are working against me. Trying to compel me to believe that what I want for myself is of a necessity wrong—" she paused, biting her lip.

"Who?" Geoff asked, his voice staccato. "Any idea?"

"No, it's all underground. I mean, I may have an idea—but not enough to take any action about. And there are other things as well—"

Geoff took her hand in a warm, comforting grasp.

"Go on, spill it !" he advised encouragingly.

It was impossible to tell him the whole story very briefly, but at least she made everything as clear as possible—the odd arrangement between the two brothers about Edgar's designs, her belief that not even his wife knew of this. The leakage of information, her conviction that Stapleton's knew far more about Chalfont's financial position than they ought to. Even Jervis's feeling that he was almost in a position to solve who the culprit was. But about his statement that if he and Eleanor were to be married, there would be no more problems, she said nothing. Geoff, she was sure, would not only resent that, but find it unpleasantly significant—

"And he, Stapleton, said that he thought it was because someone wanted to make them think you weren't worth while taking over?" Geoff pondered. "And you said it might be that someone was hoping to damage your reputation so that they might buy you up more cheaply. How did he take that?"

"Just that it was all part of a scheme to increase the enmity between the two firms," Eleanor explained.

"By someone who thought they could do better with you in control than with a hardheaded lot like the Stapletons?" Geoff suggested. "Eleanor, don't think I'm underrating you, but honestly, are you a good enough business woman to be able to control that firm practically on your own? I mean, even if you left out any idea of marriage—which you aren't going to—" with a reassuring tightening of his hand, "and gave absolutely everything to it. Could you make a go of it?"

"No, I couldn't," Eleanor answered tersely. "Oh, Geoff, you don't know what a relief it is to say that! It's been worrying me so much. I can honestly say that I was a good secretary to Uncle Simon, but that's a very different thing from being responsible for running the whole business myself. I do know quite a lot about the business side, of course, but even so, not enough. And as for the practical aspect, the processes, and perhaps even more, the assessing of the market we supply, I just don't even *start*! So I've got to find someone who, like Uncle Simon, has all that at his fingertips, and whom I can trust. And I think the only way in which his interests and the firm's can be one is if he is a partner. Don't you think I'm right?"

"It makes sense to me," Geoff said soberly. "And I only wish to goodness I could be the one to help you out. But there it is—I don't know the first thing about any sort of business except my own, and I don't think

I've got the sort of brain that could learn, even if there was anyone to teach me, which there isn't. So what? Or rather, who?"

Eleanor shook her head.

"I don't know," she sighed. "It won't be easy to find the right person. But one thing I'm sure of—it won't be anyone at all unless Uncle Edgar is made to see that something like this has got to be done!" She fell silent, longing for the assurance that only Geoff could give her.

"And you believe that if we got married, he'd be more likely to see it?" Geoff said thoughtfully. "Yes, I think you could be right. So we'll go ahead with the date we originally planned, shall we—the twenty-fifth?"

"Yes," Eleanor said breathlessly. "The twenty-fifth!"

Geoff put his arm round her and drew her close. She laid her head on his shoulder, her heart more at ease than it had been for many weeks. And this feeling of peace and security lasted for the rest of the day and over to the Sunday. It was only just as she was leaving that Geoff made a disconcerting suggestion.

"Eleanor, you don't think it's your Uncle Edgar who has been putting all this gossip about, do you?"

Eleanor hesitated.

"I have wondered," she confessed. "Because he's so terribly against any form of change. But somehow I can't believe it. I mean he's such a—well, really a simple, straightforward sort of person. And for him to have started these rumours just wouldn't be in character, would it? It's such an unpleasantly oblique and under-handed approach—no, I can't believe it, Geoff. But what made you think it was a possibility?"

"Well, actually, young Celia," Geoff explained. "She'd very definitely got something on her mind that was worrying her. Didn't you realise that the kid was on edge all the time she was here?"

"Yes, I did," Eleanor said slowly. It was really quite useless to deny it, but she was determined not to let Geoff guess the real reason why Celia had been so tense if she could possibly help it. "And you mean you think she's got some idea about her father—?"

"I know that she's having a pretty thin time of it at home, one way and another," Geoff said grimly. "Everlasting rows between her parents—there could be something there. But what makes me think it could be something about the firm that's worrying her is that she seemed quite all right when she first got here, but when you came—well, if it wasn't that it sounded so far-fetched, I'd say she felt almost guilty because she's naturally loyal to her father and yet she doesn't feel you're getting a square deal. Or am I making mountains out of molehills?"

"I wouldn't like to say," Eleanor said quite truthfully. "But anyway, I'm not going to waste any time before tackling Uncle Edgar, so perhaps when I have, it may settle whatever it is that's worrying Celia—" She knew quite well that it would do nothing of the sort, but she was determined not to betray her young cousin's pathetic little secret if it could possibly be avoided.

*   *   *

Eleanor wasn't looking forward to the interview with her uncle, but that was, to her mind, just one more reason why the sooner it was over, the better. Otherwise she would simply brood about it until, perhaps, she might even lose her nerve.

So as soon as she reached the works on the Monday morning, she rang through on the house phone and asked him to come and see her as soon as possible. There was a little pause, and she thought she heard the swift intake of his breath as if he wasn't too pleased at the request. The curt way in which he said he would be over in an hour's time gave substance to that possibility. Then, in an apologetic, almost ingratiating way, oddly at variance with his earlier manner, he explained that he had just started rather a ticklish process which would take about that time.

"Very well," Eleanor replied with determined cheerfulness. "Round about nine-fifteen, then."

There was no answer from the other end except a click as the instrument was hung up. No, Eleanor thought ruefully as she, too, cradled the instrument, it wasn't going to be easy or pleasant!

But when Edgar arrived, he showed no signs whatever of resenting having been sent for. Indeed, there was something almost benign about his smiling face.

"Now, what is it, my dear?" he asked genially. "No trouble of any sort, is there?"

"No, just I want you to be the first one to hear some good news—and then I want to discuss the effect that it will have—"

Edgar said nothing, but his eyes narrowed and his spare frame tensed. Eleanor, gaining courage from the sparkle of Geoff's ring as her hands lay loosely linked before her on the desk, came to the point.

"Geoff and I are getting married on the twenty-fifth of August."

"What!"

He sprang to his feet, his hands clenching and unclenching as he glared down at her. She had never seen him in such a rage before and it took all her courage simply to sit there and meet his eyes steadily.

"What is there about that to surprise you, Uncle Edgar?" she asked coolly. "Surely you must know it's the date we settled on long ago."

"But since then—since then—" Edgar stammered, and licked his lips as if they were suddenly dry. "You promised—"

"I promised only one thing," Eleanor told him steadily. "To marry Geoff on the twenty-fifth of August, and nothing and nobody is going to prevent me from doing that."

"But—but your promise to Simon—" Edgar protested. "Not to get married for a year—"

"No, I didn't promise that," Eleanor insisted. "Nor did Uncle Simon ask me to. Simply, in a letter which I didn't have until after his death, he asked me to *consider* deferring my marriage. Well, I have considered it, and I've come to the conclusion that it's neither reasonable nor necessary for me to make such a sacrifice."

"But you can't betray a dead man's wish like that!" Edgar shouted, running his fingers through his sparse hair. "It's not decent!"

"That's quite absurd," Eleanor told him bluntly. "If Uncle Simon had felt as strongly as that about it, he'd have made it a condition in his will. But he didn't. He left me completely free to make my own decision. And

I've done so. And please do sit down again, Uncle Edgar, because we've a lot to talk about."

He sank down in the chair and covered his face with his hands. He was trembling all over, and for the first time in her life, Eleanor felt a repugnance for him. Surely there was something wrong about a man who could go to pieces so readily—

"Well?" he asked in a subdued voice. "What is it?"

"Just this, Uncle," Eleanor said steadily, "I know now that I can't possibly take Uncle Simon's place. It's too big, too demanding a job—"

"It wouldn't be—if only you'd give up this absurd idea of marrying a—a second-rater who's obviously after your money."

Eleanor stiffened. If the interview was to be kept from developing into a vulgar brawl, she must make a stand now.

"You're forgetting that Geoff and I were engaged long before I became Uncle Simon's heiress," Eleanor said coldly. "And now, leaving personalities entirely out of it, this is what I propose—either that you must relieve me of more work than Uncle Simon needed to ask of you, or we must find a third partner—now!"

Again Edgar was on his feet.

"You can't do that, Eleanor—I forbid it." He was almost raving in his anger. "This has always been Chalfont's and—"

"Uncle Edgar, please sit down and—"

"I'm damned if I will," he shouted, the last shred of his self-control going. "Not until you see sense! So just listen to me, young woman! I may not have as big a financial interest in the firm as you have, but—"

"But you have got as big an interest—or very nearly, haven't you, Uncle Edgar?" Eleanor said quietly. "The accounts of the royalties you've been paid for your designs—"

"Well?" he demanded truculently. "What of it? The firm's done very well out of me, hasn't it? In fact, without my work—"

"But you are a partner of the firm," Eleanor pointed out. "So, in effect, you've been paid twice for the same work."

"If that arrangement suited Simon, it ought to be good enough for you," he flung at her.

"I'm sorry, but it isn't," Eleanor told him.

"You mean, unless I toe the line and do exactly what I'm told, you're not going to renew the agreement?" he demanded, poking his head forward as if to see her more clearly.

"I hope it won't be necessary for me to do that," she murmured, wishing it didn't sound so much like blackmail.

"You can't afford to do it," he declared arrogantly. "The firm needs my work! You don't believe that, do you? Well, it's true—"

"All the same, there are some prices that are too big to pay—" Eleanor began, but he waved her away.

"Not for some things," he insisted. "Not for something I've just finished working on! Wait, and I'll show you!"

He darted out of the room, leaving Eleanor to wonder what this stranger, who was also Uncle Edgar, had got up his sleeve that made him so unfamiliarly confident.

CHAPTER VIII

ELEANOR had not long to wait. Edgar Chalfont was back in her room in a few minutes carrying a small and shabby leather case which he set down on Eleanor's desk.

He flicked open the locks and took out a small tissue paper wrapped object which he handed to Eleanor.

"Now then!" he said exultantly. "Take a look at that —and own up I'm right! You can't do without me—on my own terms, young woman!"

Silently Eleanor removed the wrappings and involuntarily caught her breath.

In her hands lay the most exquisite coffee cup she had ever seen.

The inside of it was painted with pale gold that just

lapped over the rim to border the outside. That was beautiful, but it was the outer surface that had taken her breath away.

It was vibrant ruby red in colour and over its lambent flame lay a delicate tracery of more gold so that the effect was of jewels set in gold.

For a moment she forgot everything else as, lost in the sheer fascination of the beautiful thing she held, she caressed the perfect outline of the cup.

"Utterly lovely!" she breathed—and was brought back to earth by Edgar's triumphant, crowing laugh.

"You see?" he wagged an admonitory finger at her. "You can't afford to ignore the old man, can you? Well, can you?" he repeated impatiently as Eleanor did not reply. "Don't you see what this means to the firm? An advance in technique like this—it's worth thousands —perhaps hundreds of thousands! And it's *mine*! Do you understand? Mine—not the firm's!" And he rubbed his hands together in a gloating way.

Eleanor laid the cup down with hands that shook a little.

"It's the most beautiful thing I've ever seen," she admitted—indeed, she had no choice but to do so. "A new process?"

"Entirely new," Edgar nodded like a mandarin. "*My* process! And one about which I've no intention of giving you an explanation except to say that it's obtained by the use of new ingredients which have only been available comparatively recently. And now, no more beating about the bush, Eleanor. I want—I intend to have—a similar contract with you as I had with Simon about the use of my copyrights—"

"Just a minute, Uncle," Eleanor said far more calmly than she really felt. "I want to know a little more before we get down to the question of contracts. Oh, not details of your process, but other points."

"Well?" Edgar asked suspiciously.

"Can you get the same effect in other colours?"

For answer, Edgar unwrapped two other cups, a sapphire blue one and an emerald green.

"I call them my Jewel Series," he announced, his eyes feasting on the beautiful things.

"A very good name," Eleanor said matter-of-factly. "Now, most important of all, is it an expensive process?"

Edgar chuckled delightedly.

"You've got your wits about you, haven't you, Eleanor? No, that's the incredible thing about it. It's cheaper than our normal processes—or rather, it would be mass-produced. Naturally these prototypes cost more to produce. But I've gone very carefully into the figures, and I'm satisfied that we could undercut anything Stapleton's can produce and show a very nice profit into the bargain!"

"Yes?" Eleanor said abstractedly. How odd, she was thinking, that Uncle Edgar had always laid such emphasis on being so completely unbusinesslike, and yet now he was showing just how false a picture that had been. It was rather frightening—all the more so because Eleanor knew that, in fairness to the firm, she must agree to the manufacture of these lovely things—and that it would have to be on Edgar's terms. Anxiously she sought for and found a possible reason for delaying the signing of a new contract with her uncle. "You've taken out a patent for the process?"

"Well—" for the first time that unsure, even furtive expression which was so much more in keeping with the man Eleanor had always known showed in his face. "I've sent off all the necessary details to the Patent Agency which looks after these things for me. I expect to hear from them any day now."

Eleanor nodded.

"Let me know when you hear from them, will you?" she requested, and significantly pushed the ruby cup gently towards him.

Edgar stared at her incredulously.

"You little fool, don't you realise you can't afford to take that sort of attitude with me?" he demanded shrilly. "This has got to be put on the market—you can't afford not to, and you know it—"

"I've already told you, there are some prices which are too big to pay," Eleanor reminded him bluntly. "But while we're discussing in this rather unpleasantly threatening way what I can or can't afford, isn't there another side to it?"

"Another side?" Edgar repeated sharply. "What do you mean?"

"Just this, Uncle Edgar," Eleanor said steadily. "The firm has done very well out of your designs. I admit it because it's undeniable. But *you've* done very well out of the firm, haven't you, Uncle Edgar?"

"What if I have?" he demanded truculently. "I've earned every penny."

"That could well be," Eleanor agreed. "It probably is. All the same, the firm has provided you with a market for your designs. Just supposing that market didn't exist. What would you do then with your designs, Uncle Edgar?"

She hated herself for saying it, for she felt that she was lowering herself to Edgar's standards—and they didn't stop far short of sheer blackmail. Yet, not only in self-defence, but because she felt reasonably sure that it was the only language he would understand, what else could she have said?

"What would I do?" he ran his fingers through his thinning hair until it stood on end. "What would I do?" he repeated. His jaw dropped and his face puckered in a preposterously childish way. It was a painfully incongruous change from his earlier cocksure manner. "I—I don't quite know," he admitted.

"Well, there's one thing you've got to remember, Uncle Edgar," Eleanor spoke firmly, but she felt sick at heart and only wished to end this interview as quickly as possible. "Both you and I are bound by the terms of the partnership agreement not to take on any work outside the firm by which we could earn money. Do you see what that means? You are relying on this firm—on me —to take your work, because if that isn't so, you can't sell your ideas to anyone else—"

"As if I would!" Edgar exploded self-righteously. "I've never been anything but loyal to this firm, and I never shall be. No, indeed! It's your loyalty that is in question!"

"Because I won't allow myself to be bullied—and it comes to that—into postponing my marriage, let alone give up the idea of marriage altogether?" Eleanor asked. "That's what you feel most strongly about, isn't it? But you've got things the wrong way round. It just isn't decent for the dead or for the living to impose their will on others against their true interests. And that's what you want to do."

"No, that isn't true, Eleanor," Edgar said earnestly. "Both Simon and I have never had anything but your true interests at heart."

"Just as you had Aunt Helen's?" Eleanor asked gravely, and knew from the sudden twitch of his lips that her shot had hit home. He hadn't known that she had heard that old story, and her knowledge made him uneasy.

"There is no similarity—" he began angrily, but Eleanor shook her head.

"Oh, but there is, Uncle Edgar. Both times, Chalfont men wanted their own way and they put what they felt was the firm's needs before the needs of human beings. Aunt Helen was persuaded to wreck her own life. I'm not going to do that. Make no mistake, Uncle Edgar!"

His lips parted petulantly.

"You're making things very difficult for me—"

"Not as difficult as they have been made for me," Eleanor said stoutly. "Surely you can see that?"

"Surely you can see that if only you would give all your devotion to the firm which, I might point out, has kept you in comfort all your life, then all our troubles would be over! Not only could we keep it going until my boy is able to play his part, but if we take up this new process of mine, we'll be utterly and permanently independent of any offer Stapleton's care to make. In fact, more than likely, we'll be able to break them because we'll command the entire market—"

His voice rose to a note of hysterical exultation, and Eleanor found herself wondering if he was quite sane.

But whether he was or not, of one thing she could be quite sure. The driving force of Edgar Chalfont's life was hatred—hatred of his rivals, hatred taken to a point where he wanted to do nothing less than ruin them completely.

What she didn't know was whether it was hatred based entirely on business rivalry—or whether there was something more personal in it than that. She could only make a guess at that, but she knew that from that moment she must do everything in her power to keep her uncle's vindictiveness from achieving its ends.

That, oddly, made her his enemy and, even though they wouldn't know it, the Stapletons' ally. Even more strange was the fact that she could accept such a state of affairs as being inevitable—and perfectly natural.

*   *   *

Edgar had only left her for a few minutes when Eleanor had a call on the house telephone from the Welfare Officer asking if she could spare a few minutes.

"It's about the firm's annual 'do,' Miss Chalfont," Mrs. Vereker explained. "But I'd like to discuss it with you, actually, rather than on the telephone."

"By all means," Eleanor agreed. "I can spare you time now if that suits you, Mrs. Vereker."

"I'll be right along," Mrs. Vereker promised cheerfully.

Eleanor sat deep in thought for several moments. She liked and trusted Mrs. Vereker, a cheerful, middle-aged woman who had a gift for gaining people's confidence and co-operation and for smoothing out difficulties. It wasn't very difficult for Eleanor to decide what was probably on Mrs. Vereker's mind now, and she tried to make up her mind just what her own feelings were about the problem she thought was going to be presented to her.

When Mrs. Vereker arrived, Eleanor greeted her with a smile and indicated the chair on the opposite side of the desk from her own.

"Now, what is it, Mrs. Vereker?" she asked pleasantly. "Something not going quite smoothly?"

"I wouldn't say that, Miss Chalfont," Mrs. Vereker replied. "I mean, the affair's only a few weeks off, so naturally, all the arrangements are made, and seeing Mr. Pavitt's in charge, there won't be any hitches. No, what's troubling him and me is whether, in view of Mr. Simon's death, we ought to have it at all. Out of respect for him, so to speak."

"Yes, I see," Eleanor said thoughtfully. "Are there a lot of people who feel that way?"

"Quite a few," Mrs. Vereker told her. "Mainly the older ones. Mind you, they'd be sorry not to have it, but they feel it's asking rather a lot of the family, so soon after—well, you see what I mean. They want you to feel free to cancel it if you like."

"How very thoughtful," Eleanor said gratefully. "And what's your own feeling, Mrs. Vereker?"

"Well, I'd be the last one to want to hurt anyone's feelings, but I can't help remembering that the party was Mr. Simon's idea—"

"Yes, that's what I was thinking," Eleanor nodded. "What does Mr. Edgar say?"

"Well, I've only got this second hand from Mr. Pavitt," Mrs. Vereker said cautiously. "But it appears he's no objection—provided there are a few alterations in the list of guests—"

"Have you got the list with you?" Eleanor asked, and it was handed to her in silence.

It was an alphabetical list, and Eleanor turned the pages until she came to the letter 'S'.

Always before the Stapleton family had been invited, just as at a later date in the year, they invited the Chalfonts to their annual affair. It was a conventional gesture less of friendship than of expediency—neither family was willing to admit that they might have any cause for fear of the other. If Eleanor had given it a thought she would have decided that embarrassing though such a situation might be, it had gone on too long to be suddenly stopped.

Her Uncle Edgar evidently didn't feel the same way. The names of Mr. and Mrs. Stapleton, Jervis, his sister and her husband had been so heavily scored out that in one or two places the pen had cut through the paper.

"Yes, I see," she said quietly, and handed the list back. There was a little silence as Mrs. Vereker fidgeted slightly with the typed sheets, her eyes avoiding Eleanor's. "Yes—well, I think we go ahead with it, Mrs. Vereker. But I should like it known how much I appreciate this thoughtfulness."

"Yes, I'll make that clear, Miss Chalfont," Mrs.

Vereker said, but rather to Eleanor's surprise, she didn't immediately get up.

"Is there something else, Mrs. Vereker?" Eleanor asked patiently, reading hesitation in the face opposite to her.

"Well, yes, there is," Mrs. Vereker said diffidently. "And it's rather a personal matter—I hope you won't be offended, Miss Chalfont, but it's always been our intention to collect for a wedding present for you—and we just rather wondered if—when—" her voice trailed to silence.

"How very kind," Eleanor said steadily. "Yes, my wedding day is fixed for the twenty-fifth of August, Mrs. Vereker."

"Oh, I'm glad to hear that!" Mrs. Vereker said warmly, and then, evidently feeling she had perhaps expressed herself rather too revealingly, she got up hurriedly, thanked Eleanor for making time to see her, and hurried out of the room.

Eleanor got up, walked to the window and stared out at a passing car. So there had been gossip about the possible postponement of her wedding. Was that due to anything Uncle Edgar had said—or was it something their employees had conjured up for themselves? Well, it didn't really matter either way. She and Geoff were going to get married and that was that! Nobody was going to stop them.

When she got home that evening, however, someone else tried to do just that. After her visit to see Geoff at the hotel when he had wrenched his knee, she had written to her mother telling her of their plans. She had not expected a quick reply because there were only a few ports into which the yacht would certainly be putting and letters might have to wait several days before they were collected. All the same, she had expected a reply before now and in more than one way was relieved to have it at last. But as she read through the pages of her mother's schoolgirl sprawl, her heart sank.

"Darling, you *have* surprised me," Kitty wrote. "I mean, to think of getting married so soon after your poor uncle's death—and anyhow, I should think, seeing how tied up you must be with office work and one thing and another, that you wouldn't be able to spend time to have a honeymoon—it doesn't really seem quite fair to Geoff, does it?

"And makes me wonder something else. Of course, I know you and he have always been quite *devoted*, but have you thought, darling, how difficult it can be for a man when his wife is the one with the money while he hasn't two sixpences to rub together? Forgive me, honey, but honestly, in these new circumstances, don't you think it might be wise to wait for a bit until you see how things work out?

"In any case, I'm afraid I couldn't possibly get back in time for your wedding—and it would look a bit queer if I wasn't there, wouldn't it? So all things considered, wouldn't it be a good thing not to be in such a hurry?"

Eleanor laid the letter down with a hand that shook a little. How odd, she thought, that her mother had used practically the same arguments that Uncle Simon and later Uncle Edgar had used. She began to feel hemmed in—terribly lonely—

It was only as she was putting the letter back into its envelope that she realised there were two or three photographs in it. She took them out and studied them without much interest until suddenly she noticed that though they were evidently taken at different times and places, they all had something in common. In each one, the same man was standing beside her mother, smiling, a little possessive, his arm linked through hers, or, in one, round her shoulders. And on her mother's face an expression that, beyond doubt, spoke of happiness and, perhaps, a suggestion of self-satisfaction.

A serious affair? Or a shipboard flirtation? Eleanor studied the man's face more attentively. He was, she thought, probably some ten years older than her mother. A pleasant face, kindly yet strong-featured—obviously an American, both by his face and his clothes. Eleanor picked up the letter again and read the final paragraphs that she had not bothered to read before.

"I'm sending you some photographs. They may interest you since you've never met Stephanie and Greg, who are in all of them. The other man is an American business friend of Greg's—Cranmer Elliot. You'd like him.

The sort of man who takes it for granted that a woman will turn to him for support and care. He's just *made* my holiday for me—"

Eleanor smiled as she read those last two sentences. Almost word for word it was what her mother had told Jervis she thought he was like, so evidently to her it was the *beau idéal* for a man to be.

Was she right? Eleanor wondered. Of course there were times when it would be wonderful just to cast one's problems and burdens on to stronger shoulders than one's own. But for always? Surely marriage ought to mean more than one partner carrying all the cares?

Yet the description lingered in Eleanor's mind.

*　　*　　*

Just when Eleanor was reading her mother's letter, Geoff had decided that it would be a good idea to go down to the local for a drink. He'd had a pretty gruelling day of it. Business was brisk, thank heaven, but though to all intents and purposes his knee was all right now, it still stiffened and ached if it remained in one position too long—as it had done during the hours he had spent in the saddle. The short walk down to the village would, he hoped, limber it up.

But it was a walk he was destined not to take.

He was just approaching the side door of the East Pavilion which he had to pass on his way out of the grounds when the door was flung open and Celia rushed out, cannoning heavily into him.

"Hey, steady!" Geoff admonished, grabbing her firmly by the arms. "You'll have both of us over if you're not careful!"

To his surprise, she struggled violently to free herself, and Geoff realised with a sense of shock that her eyes were glassily blind. She simply didn't realise who it was that was holding her. He shook her sharply by the shoulders.

"Snap out of it, young Celia," he said authoritatively. "It's me, Geoff. No need to be scared."

"Oh—" the blank look faded from her eyes, but with it seemed to go all her strength. Geoff felt her sag limply against him, and gathering her up competently in his arms, he half led, half carried her back to the stable yard he had just left. He set her carefully on the old stone mounting block, and with stern instructions not to move, dashed upstairs to his flat and came back in an incredibly short time with a small glass in his hand.

"Sip this," he ordered, and then, seeing how the hand she meekly held out was shaking, he squatted down beside her and held the glass to her lips.

"Ough, it's strong!" she gasped, choking over the fiery spirit.

"Bring back the roses to your cheeks in no time," Geoff told her. "Go on, keep at it!"

But when, half way through the stiff shot he had poured out, she gently pushed his hand away and said "No more," he let her have her way.

"And now suppose you tell me what's happened," he suggested. "What had scared you?"

"You mean because I tried to get away when you held me?" Celia asked. "I wasn't scared, Geoff. It was just that, after what had happened, I simply couldn't *bear* any more restraint and—and frustration."

"And what had happened?" Geoff asked very quietly, because he realised now just how easy it would be to startle Celia into resentful silence when, he was convinced, what she really needed was to relieve her feelings by talking about her troubles, whatever they were. Even now he was not sure that she didn't resent his question, for she said nothing for several moments. Then it all came out in a rush.

"It was Father," she explained bitterly. "He was absolutely beastly to Dick and me—he simply wouldn't take any notice of what we told him we wanted to do— and worse than that, he told us just what he'd planned for us. And we'd got to do it, whether we wanted to or not."

"That doesn't sound like your father," Geoff objected gently. "I mean, he's always been so quiet and—well, not inclined to assert himself at all."

Celia laughed on a jarring, scornful note.

"Don't you believe it!" she told him. "Father *always* gets his own way. Not that one always realises he has until long afterwards, but somehow or other—" she stopped, frowning deeply. Then she shook her head. "I can't explain just how it happens, but I know it does. It's sort of by indirect means—no, it's no good. Either you know that he's like that or you don't. I suppose it's living with him that makes one understand." She paused a minute and then went on thoughtfully : "I bet Eleanor knows just what I mean by now!"

Geoff looked at her sharply, but made no comment on her last remark, though he could have confirmed that Celia wasn't so far out in her deductions.

"But this time, I gather, there was nothing round-about in what he said," he suggested. "He came right out into the open?"

"He certainly did!" Celia agreed emphatically. "Well, Dick and I practically forced him to. You see, we've known for a long time what we want to do. Dick wants to go on the land—Mother's people were—are—all farmers, you know. And I want to go into the works, learn everything from the bottom up and then specialise in design."

"Well, I can't see anything unreasonable in either plan," Geoff said judicially.

"Of course you can't, because you're a reasonable person with an open mind," Celia said scornfully. "But Father isn't. Not when he's made up his mind to some-thing quite different. Dick is to be the one who goes into the firm, though not until he's through at Cambridge."

"And you?" Geoff asked, and was touched at the pathos in her voice as she replied :

"Oh, me! I just don't matter! Father doesn't believe in girls having careers. He'd like me to stay at home and help Mother—just fritter my time away! Oh, I don't suppose he'd mind me playing about with a box of paints just for my own amusement. But not anything serious."

"I don't know that I'm altogether in favour of girls having careers myself," Geoff said slowly. "It can lead to—difficulties."

Celia's eyes widened slightly and seemed to Geoff to darken in an odd way.

"Are you talking about you and Eleanor?" she asked bluntly. "Are there—difficulties?"

Geoff stood erect, suddenly conscious that squatting down like that beside Celia had made his knee ache viciously.

"No, I'm not," he said shortly. "There might have been difficulties—only we're not allowing there to be. We're getting married on the twenty-fifth of August."

"But—" Celia gave a little gasp and counted up on her fingers—"that's only a few weeks off!"

"What of it?" Geoff asked indifferently. "It's just about the date we've always planned."

"Yes, but with all that's happened—Uncle Simon and Eleanor taking his place, I should have thought—" Celia began, and stopped short at the sight of the annoyance in Geoff's expression.

"Now don't you start on that line!" he said irritably. "We've had enough of that already—"

"From Father?" Celia asked swiftly.

For a moment Geoff pressed his lips firmly together. Then he nodded.

"Among others," he said briefly. "So, young Celia, you can just lay off, if you please!"

Celia stood up and stood fidgeting from one foot to the other as if she couldn't make up her mind what to do. She looked so forlorn that Geoff forgot his irritation and putting his arm round her, gave her a friendly hug.

"Now look here, Celia, Eleanor and I have got out of this bother by cutting the Gordian knot—taking the law into our own hands, in other words. I don't see why both Dick and you can't do the same thing."

"How?" Celia asked with interest.

"Well, as regards Dick, if I were him, I'd go through with it at university. Then, if he's really keen, he could go to a farm somewhere—possibly one belonging to your mother's people—and learn from the bottom up. He'd have to be content to living on a tight budget for a bit, but if he's really keen, wouldn't that be worth it?"

"Yes, it would," Celia agreed. "And me?"

Geoff pondered.

"Well, you've offered your skill to the family firm— at least, to your father. Does Eleanor know anything about this ambition of yours."

"Oh yes, I told her—and she was quite agreeable.

She even said she'd see about persuading Father. But I don't think she's done anything about it," Celia said dejectedly.

"Well, it may not have occurred to you, but Eleanor's got quite a lot on her own mind at present," Geoff explained. "And anyway, if your father feels so strongly about it, I doubt if she'd be able to persuade him. I mean, she's the senior partner, but this is a family matter. In any case—" he paused, wondering if what was in his mind was a wise thing to say or whether it would just make more trouble. He decided to chance it. "Hasn't it occurred to you that it might be a good idea to stand on your own feet? Not rely on other people to give you a chance, but to make your own chance? Why not launch out by sending some of your designs to—" he stopped short, suddenly realising where this was leading. The most obvious place to send specimens of her work, since Chalfont's didn't appear to want it, was Stapleton's. And he could imagine just what a riot that would cause.

"To some other firm?" Celia finished thoughtfully. "Yes, I think you've got something there, Geoff. Thank you!"

Gently she disengaged herself from his arm, gave him a smile of such piercing sweetness that Geoff's jaw dropped slightly—and walked slowly back to her home.

Geoff stood stock still for several moments, his thoughts in a whirl. There was something different about Celia—something he'd never appreciated before—

At last he shrugged his shoulders.

"Just, rather belatedly, she's growing up, I suppose," he explained the revelation to himself.

But it didn't satisfy him. It didn't seem to go far enough.

*   *   *

There was so much to do that to Eleanor the weeks flashed past. Nor was it only that her day's work kept her so busy. There were the arrangements to be made for the wedding which meant various shopping expeditions, though she had decided not to wear formal bridal white. That seemed unsuitable since she and Geoff had decided that though they wanted to be married in church, it should be a very quiet affair. In fact, hole-and-corner was the sneering way in which Edgar referred to it when he knew what their plans were.

"As if she was ashamed of what she's doing," he remarked bitterly to his wife. "And so she should be, the little fool, throwing herself away on a ne'er-do-well like young Baynes!"

Alice Chalfont didn't reply, but the glance she gave her husband was both troubled and perplexed. There was something very odd about Edgar these days. He had changed so very much.

She picked up the letter which Eleanor had written, inviting both of them and Celia and Richard to the wedding. Eleanor had also asked her uncle to give her away.

"Of course, we'll have to go," Alice said, but there was a tentative note in her voice.

"Indeed?" Edgar replied ironically. "I see no reason at all why we should do any such thing. And most certainly I shall forbid the children to go! As for giving her away—to make such a request in the circumstances is nothing short of sheer impertinence on her part!"

It was, of course, nothing of the sort. Simply, Eleanor had felt obliged to observe the convention of making the request of her nearest male relative—and drew a sigh of relief when she received his refusal. It left her free to make a similar request of her Aunt Helen.

"Certainly, my dear," Helen promised unhesitatingly. "That is if, as I suppose is the case, Edgar has already refused to take it on?"

"Yes, he has," Eleanor acknowledged. "But how did you guess, Aunt Helen?"

The smile her aunt gave her was very kindly.

"Because, for one thing, I was quite sure you would have both the tact and the good manners to have approached Edgar first—it is really his job, of course. But then I know my brother—" the smile faded and she sighed deeply. "He's always so sure that he knows best that when anyone opposes him—yes, I know all about it, my dear, Edgar has been singularly indiscreet, I'm afraid."

"But you don't think I'm wrong not to postpone getting married, do you?" Eleanor asked anxiously. More than anything else in the world at that moment she wanted the assurance that only an older, more experienced person could give her.

Helen covered her niece's hand with her own and clasped it firmly, but her voice was not quite steady as she replied :

"My dear, I believe that you—that everyone—should follow their heart. To do anything else means a lifetime of regret."

A brief silence fell between them. Then they began to discuss the practical aspects of the wedding and the moment of emotion had passed. But later, when she had left her aunt, Eleanor realised uneasily that her question had not really been answered.

*   *   *

As well as buying various items for her trousseau, Eleanor felt she must get a new dress for the firm's "do" as it was usually called. And perhaps because, like most other girls, she had dreamed of a white wedding dress, and was now having to forget her dream, she was easily persuaded that one particular evening dress was the only one she could possibly buy. Needless to say, it was the most expensive one, but she didn't need the assurance of the *vendeuse* to know that it suited her as no other dress did.

It was a full-length dress made of two layers of nylon both of which were basically a pale primrose yellow in colour. But the transparent outer layer of material was patterned with shadowy roses in a deeper shade of yellow and their green leaves. The neck was softly finished with a cleverly pleated fichu of the same material. And it fitted Eleanor perfectly without any alterations at all. That finally settled the matter, for there was very little time now before the "do"—and only a week longer before her wedding day.

Yet no thought of her wedding day was in her mind as, wearing her pretty dress, she left the West Pavilion and walked along the covered arcade which led to the big house where the "do" was always held. Rather she was filled with a conviction that something wonderful and exciting would happen *tonight*. She could not even guess what it might be nor understand why she should feel so sure about it, but it was just as real as, when she was a child, she had believed so firmly that there was such a thing as Magic, just round the corner, if only you could catch up with it! And no amount of disappointments had ever quite robbed her of that childish belief.

No one had arrived yet, of course, not even the Edgar Chalfonts or Geoff, so she had time to make sure that everything was just so.

The dance was to be held in the Great Drawing Room—a somewhat ostentatiously big room which, these days, was the principal display room of the Chalfont Museum. For tonight, all the glass cases had been removed and packed away in a smaller room. Flowers had been arranged in corners and alcoves, a dais had been placed at one end of the room for the band, already there and tuning up. Eleanor had a word with the leader and then went to leave the light cloak she had slung over her shoulders in the room which was being used as the cloakroom.

When she got back to the drawing room, Edgar and Alice were there together with Dick and the young partner he had brought. Of Celia there was no sign.

"She won't be long," Alice explained with a diffidence that was unusual in her. "She had a telephone call just before we left."

But Celia had still not arrived when it became time for the family to line up to receive their guests. By now, however, Geoff, more than usually handsome in his formal black and white, had come, and despite Edgar's scowl, he stood beside Eleanor in the receiving line.

Now there was a steady flow of guests, increasing to a flood as coachloads of employees arrived. Punctually, half an hour after the official time of commencement, the band stopped playing soft background music and swung into an infectiously gay dance tune. Immediately, two circles, the one facing the other, formed up, the girls on the inner ring, the men on the outer. This, too, was the custom on these occasions. Nothing like a Paul Jones for breaking the ice! Why, it might mean that one of the newest and youngest little messenger girls would dance with a departmental manager—and nobody could be stuffy and formal after that. It set the mood for the evening.

Round and round went the two rings, the girls in one direction, the men in the other. Eleanor had Mrs. Vereker on her right, and a pretty little girl from the typing pool on her left.

Suddenly the music stopped—and everyone stood still.

"Good evening!" said a deep, slightly amused voice that Eleanor instantly recognised. "May I have the pleasure—?"

And, too startled to protest, Eleanor allowed herself to be swung into the dance in the arms of—Jervis Stapleton.

CHAPTER IX

IT was fortunate that Jervis was an extremely good dancer, for in her bewildered surprise at his presence, Eleanor missed a step and stumbled badly. Instantly Jervis's arms tightened round her and she felt herself steadied so swiftly that she was able to regain her balance before anyone else could be aware of her clumsiness.

But neither of them spoke, not even for Jervis to murmur the conventional apology as if it had been his fault or for Eleanor to have thanked him for his assistance. But while the incident appeared to make no difference to Jervis's easy style of dancing, Eleanor felt herself growing more and more rigid in his arms.

Despite her strong feeling that it had been both foolish and undignified of her uncle to take the Stapletons off their list of guests, she had decided to let the matter slide. There were already too many differences of opinion between Edgar and herself. To make an issue of this might well be the last straw.

Yet now here she was, dancing with Jervis Stapleton.

The rest of the family might be here as well, though somehow she didn't think so—and that not just because so far she hadn't seen any of them. There had come an instinctive conviction that she really knew how it was Jervis was here. But she had to know for sure, so as soon as she had regained her breath she said quietly:

"Mr. Stapleton, when we reach the doors that lead to the terrace, will you please come out there with me? There are things we have to discuss."

"By all means," Jervis promised as equably as to suggest that her request didn't come as a surprise to him.

When they reached the open doors, Jervis skilfully extricated the two of them from the rest of the dancers with the minimum amount of fuss and led Eleanor out on to the terrace. He seemed to know his way about, for he steered her towards the short flight of steps that led to the garden and from there to the sequestered rose garden where additional seats and chairs had been put out for that evening. Fortunately it was still too early in the evening for the rest of the guests to be interested in anything except dancing.

"Here?" Jervis indicated a swinging garden seat. He flicked the cushions perfunctorily with his handkerchief and very thankfully Eleanor sat down, her legs suddenly refusing to support her another second.

Jervis, however, remained standing, a tall, commanding figure. Not particularly handsome, perhaps—certainly not as handsome as Geoff, and yet with something about him that held a very definite appeal—

"The sort of man who feels it's natural for a woman to turn to a man for support and care—"

The echo of her mother's words rang in her ears, but impatiently she pushed them from her. This was no time or place for sentiment—and anyway, such a relationship wasn't possible between them, of all people!

"I do wish you'd sit down," Eleanor said with a faintly querulous note in her voice. "It gives me a crick in my neck looking up at you!"

"And," she might have added, *"it gives me an inferiority complex! I'm sure you feel you're completely master of the situation, and I shall end up thinking the same thing if you keep on towering over me!"*

Obediently Jervis sat down, but he still left it to Eleanor to begin the conversation she had been the one to suggest. She drew a deep breath. If he thought she was afraid of him—

"Mr. Stapleton, how does it come that you are here?" she asked quietly.

The moonlight was bright enough for her to see that there was no surprise in his face at her question. It was, in fact, completely expressionless as he said easily :

"I was invited to come."

"Yes?" Eleanor looked at him steadily, her head slightly on one side. "By whom?"

"By one of your guests," he explained without a hint of embarrassment. "I came as her partner."

"Yes, I imagined it must be something like that," Eleanor said rather coldly. "But didn't it occur to you that in the circumstances, it was in rather questionable taste for you to do so?"

"You mean, in the circumstances of none of us having received our usual invitations to the affair this year?" Jervis asked coolly. "No, I don't think that's the word I'd use. I admit to considerable curiosity—and with that, a determination to find out just why the change in procedure. And also," he added thoughtfully, "to find out who was responsible for it—you, your uncle—or both of you!"

Standing up or sitting down, he *was* master of the situation, Eleanor thought ruefully. She had attempted to take the war into the enemy's camp and somehow he had contrived to rout her. Well, there was only one thing to do—tell the truth if only because she was quite sure that he would know if she didn't—and that would be intolerable.

"My uncle was responsible for scoring your names off the list," she said quietly, and was surprised to find what a relief it was to explain to him. "I was responsible for not insisting that they should be replaced. I wish—I've wished all along—that it had seemed possible to do so, but I'm not going to try to excuse myself—"

"I think in all probability that your reason for not taking a stand was that there was already too much trouble brewing between your uncle and yourself for you to make a stand about a comparatively trivial matter like this," he suggested, and Eleanor had to swallow hard because of the lump that the kindness in the way he spoke had brought to her throat.

"Something like that," she admitted, too tired to appreciate that confiding in Jervis, of all people, put her loyalty to her uncle into question. But something of that idea must have been in Jervis's mind, for he said gently :

"I wish I could do something to help—but of all people, I'm most handicapped! Still, there is one thing —having got an answer to my question, I think I'd better go before I make trouble for you—as I certainly will, once your uncle sees me."

But this Eleanor would not have.

"You ought to have been asked, in the way you always have been," she insisted. "It will help me to feel you've forgiven me if you will stay—"

"But, my dear girl, there's no question of forgiveness," Jervis protested. "You were in a very awkward situation and you took what seemed to be the best way out at the time. No one can do more than that!" He hesitated. "All the same, I'm not sure I hadn't better go, because I don't want to get—my partner—into trouble."

"It was Celia, wasn't it?" Eleanor asked, and Jervis looked genuinely surprised.

"Now what on earth makes you think that?" he asked.

"Partly because she was late coming over here—which could have been so that her parents didn't know you were coming—" she looked questioningly at Jervis, who nodded. "And for another, I don't quite know. An instinct, perhaps."

"A very sound one," Jervis told her. And then, almost to himself : "I don't think I'm betraying her confidence when I say that—she had what evidently seemed to her a very good reason for asking me."

"Yes, she must have done," Eleanor agreed simply. "Otherwise I don't think she'd have risked getting into trouble with her father, as she certainly would if—"

"Ah, but don't you see, that was all part of a deep-laid scheme," Jervis explained. "I wouldn't tell you about this, but I think you may be able to help. As you know, Celia has artistic leanings with special reference to pottery and design."

"Yes, I know, she told me," Eleanor admitted. "I ought to have tackled Uncle Edgar before now about that as well—"

"I doubt if it would have done any good," Jervis said dryly. "Because, in fact, Celia tackled him herself, and at the same time her brother told his father that he had no intention of ever coming into the firm. There appears to have been a first-class row—"

"Yes, I'm afraid there would be," Eleanor said, dismayed at the picture his words conjured up. "But in that case, why on earth did she—"

"Because she got it all worked out in that ingenious little mind of hers that if she presented her father with an even less acceptable plan, he might change his mind about having her working for Chalfont's," Jervis explained. "In other words, she suggested that I should offer her a job."

"What!" Eleanor exclaimed.

"I know, incredible, isn't it?" Jervis said coolly. "And in order, to quote Pooh-Bah, to give verisimilitude to an otherwise bald and unconvincing narrative, she asked me to partner her here tonight. I really ought to have refused, no doubt, but as I said, I had my own reasons for coming—"

"Your reason for such an impertinence is of no importance whatever!" said a furious voice, and Jervis stood quietly up to face Edgar Chalfont, whose approach neither of them had been aware of, so deep had they been in their own conversation. "The fact is that you're here and you've no right to be! So get out—or I'll have you chucked out!"

Jervis shrugged his shoulders as he turned to Eleanor, who had also stood up.

"I think perhaps it will save bother if I do," he said gently. "Forgive me if I've—"

"No!" Eleanor laid a detaining hand on his coat sleeve and turned defiantly to Edgar. "Mr. Stapleton is here as my guest, Uncle Edgar. And if he's willing to after your rudeness, I should like him to stay!"

There was a soft little gasp which surprised them all. It had come from Celia who, with Geoff, had come through the archway leading to the garden. Edgar turned on them angrily.

"Get out of here!" he snarled. "At once!"

"But, Father, you've got to listen—" Celia told her father, who was now speechless with anger at this fresh defiance.

"Geoff, will you please take Celia back to the house?" Eleanor asked quietly. "There's nothing for her to bother about. Nothing at all. I can deal with everything!"

For a moment Geoff looked doubtful. Then slipping his arm through Celia's, he whispered something in her ear which appeared to persuade her to do as Eleanor wished, for she allowed herself to be led away although she looked back more than once.

"Now then!" Edgar said belligerently.

"Just a minute, Uncle, before you say anything else," Eleanor said warningly. "I want you to remember something. You took five names off our list of guests without consulting me. I need no excuse nor is there any need for me to explain why Mr. Stapleton is here without your agreement. Do you understand?"

"Why, you little—" Edgar began furiously, and his hand swung up, only to be caught and firmly held by Jervis who, in some mysterious manner, was now standing between Eleanor and Edgar. "Let go!" He struggled wildly to free himself, but Jervis held on.

"If you struggle, you'll only hurt yourself," Jervis told him coolly. "Now then, are you going to behave rationally—or do I have to frog-march you back to the house?"

For a tense moment it hung in the balance. Then, curiously, Edgar seemed to shrink into himself. Eleanor drew a deep breath. She knew what had happened. Uncle Edgar had had to acknowledge to himself that he was up against a man who, both physically and morally, was stronger than he himself was.

"All right," Edgar said sulkily. "You can let go. But only because I don't want a fuss now. But don't imagine that this is the end of this business!"

"No," Jervis agreed thoughtfully, "I rather think you're right about that!"

Edgar did not reply, but the look he gave Jervis as he left the rose garden showed pretty clearly what he was thinking and feeling. When he had gone, Eleanor sat down shakily and buried her face in her hands. After a moment's hesitation, Jervis sat down beside her and laid his hand gently on her arm.

"Don't be too put out, Eleanor. It wasn't pleasant, but I suppose it is gruelling for a man of his type to have a young woman in the position of authority he thought was going to be his own, particularly when she also happens to be his niece. But give him time. He'll adjust himself."

"Or I shall?" Eleanor asked ruefully. "No, that's just the trouble. I know that I mustn't. You see, Uncle Simon left things this way just because he knew that Uncle Edgar is—" she stopped, biting her lip.

"Is governed, in all he does, by hatred," Jervis suggested soberly. "Yes, indeed, I take his point! I suppose, by the way, you've realised that it was undoubtedly your uncle—Edgar, I mean—who let those various bits of information out so inconveniently for everyone concerned?"

"I'd come to that conclusion," Eleanor confessed. "But I've never had any proof—have you?"

"Admittedly, only the sort of proof that one gets by eliminating every other possibility," Jervis told her. "And I doubt if, in a court of law, that would hold water, even if one wanted to go so far—my dear, what is it?"

For Eleanor, to whom tears never came easily, was now weeping in a silent, heartbroken way that would have touched the stoniest of hearts—and Jervis's was not that. With a little exclamation he put his arms round her and held her close, and for a few moments Eleanor surrendered to the comforting reassurance. Then, very gently, she disengaged herself and did her best to smile.

"I'm sorry," she said ruefully. "I don't often let go like that—but I'm beginning to get so frightened— Oh, not that Uncle Edgar will do me a physical injury. I don't think he'd really have hit me just now, you know.

But it's worse than that." She paused for a moment and then went on : "You know, I don't wonder people are so critical of career women. They're hard and—and unfeminine. I know. I'm getting that way myself in sheer self-defence. It's the opposition that does it—the knowledge that you're invading a man's world and that neither they nor other women like her for it! And that makes one get still harder—oh, you don't know how I wish Uncle Simon hadn't left me everything! I'd have been so much happier as an ordinary secretary!"

"You realise, don't you, that feeling that way you'll never really get hard, don't you?" Jervis asked her. "Oh, perhaps skin deep, but not right through and through. You'll be yourself again once this trouble blows over, you'll see!"

"*If* it does blow over," Eleanor said sombrely. "I sometimes don't think it *can*!" And she thought, in a quick moment of panic, of the extraordinary hold over the firm that Uncle Edgar had because of the way in which he had been allowed to keep the copyright of his designs—but of course Jervis knew nothing about that, and she certainly could not tell him.

"I suppose you haven't thought any more of my idea of cutting the Gordian knot by—marrying me?" Jervis suggested tentatively, and felt Eleanor start.

"No, I haven't, Mr. Stapleton," she found herself speaking almost apologetically. "But I have taken your advice to heart. I don't think I told you, but both Uncle Simon and Uncle Edgar have tried to make me postpone Geoff's and my wedding day so that I could devote myself to the firm. And we've decided that we just aren't having that. So we're getting married as we planned, this month. Next week, in fact."

"I see," Jervis said consideringly. "You think that may help matters?"

"Well, it will at least make Uncle Edgar realise that other people have just as much right as he has to make decisions," Eleanor pointed out.

"Yes," Jervis said thoughtfully. "It might do that—though it seems rather an odd reason for getting married, don't you think?"

"You surely don't imagine that's the only reason—"

Eleanor began hotly, and checked herself. "No, of course you don't! But I gather you don't think it's a very good idea?"

"I don't know Baynes well enough to be able to answer that," Jervis said discreetly as he stood up. "But, please believe me when I say that I wish you—and him —the very best of good fortune."

"Thank you," Eleanor said a trifle coldly because she felt oddly chilled by his reception of her news. "And now I really think we must go in. I have a whole string of duty dances—"

"Yes, of course," Jervis agreed. "But there is just one other thing I would like to tell you—"

"Yes?" Eleanor found herself waiting tensely for what he had to say—even holding her breath.

"About young Celia," he explained matter-of-factly. "Of course I had to tell her that we couldn't take her on, no matter how good she may be. On all counts, it simply wouldn't do. I'm afraid that was rather a disappointment to her, so I compromised by telling her that if she cared to write to a friend of mine in the same line but whose works are a good many miles from here, enclosing some of her designs, I'll drop him a note so that he gives them personal attention. It would mean that unless she's silly enough to tell him that I had anything to do with it, she may be able to get round her father without there being too much trouble. I hope that's all right by you?"

"Oh, quite," Eleanor replied with brittle brightness. "It was very kind and understanding of you. And now shall we go in?"

"By all means," Jervis said equably.

*   *   *

The rest of the evening passed comparatively uneventfully, although more than one person commented to Eleanor on her uncle's appearance.

"Really, he looks quite *ill*," was the tactful way most people put it. "Of course, his brother's death must have been a great shock to him—"

"It was a shock to all of us," Eleanor replied steadily, trying not to feel that the remark held the implication that she was in some way to blame for her uncle's strained nerves. "Uncle Simon had not told anyone of his heart condition."

Then there were other people who had heard of her approaching marriage and who, even in congratulating her, contrived to convey the impression that they were surprised and even perhaps a little shocked that the wedding should follow so comparatively soon after Simon's death. And to that, Eleanor could only say that it was the date she and Geoff had decided on long ago, but even as she said it, she wondered if Uncle Edgar could in some way be at least indirectly responsible for this attitude. It would be in keeping with everything else.

Her duty dances over, Eleanor danced twice with Geoff, or rather, danced once and sat out for the second one since Geoff's knee was troubling him again.

"I'll have to have it X-rayed," he said gloomily, gently massaging the offending knee. "Brierly wanted me to when I first came home after having done it, but it seemed to be getting better, so I didn't worry. I think I'll see about having it done next week, Eleanor. It always takes a little time to get the films through, so that will just fit in. I can pamper it a bit while we're away, and then, if there's any treatment needed, I can get on with it as soon as we get back."

They had decided to spend a week in London, doing various shows—a complete change and a treat for both of them. But since they had made the necessary arrangements, they had not referred to their honeymoon to one another. Perhaps that was only natural seeing that they had made quite detailed plans for it, but now that Geoff did refer to it again, Eleanor felt unaccountably ill at ease. It was absurd, of course, but she felt as if the man with whom she had promised to spend the rest of her life was a stranger instead of Geoff whom she had known and loved so long. Hastily she pushed the thought to the back of her mind and asked him if he was very heavily booked for the following week.

"Pretty well," he told her. "But young Celia is going to help me out. She's quite a good little rider and reasonably sound as an instructor. And that reminds me—about Stapleton coming here as her guest. If her father finds out—"

"There's no reason why he should," Eleanor declared. "I told Uncle Edgar he'd come as *my* guest, so if there's any more trouble, it will fall on my shoulders, not Celia's."

"Yes, I thought that was what you meant to do when you said so emphatically that there was nothing for Celia to worry about. She didn't quite like letting you in for it, but I pointed out that since you obviously didn't want her butting in, it could only be because you felt it would make things worse if she did. She took a bit of convincing, but I'm thankful to say I managed it in the end."

"Thankful?" Eleanor asked sharply.

"Yes, because I feel I'm partly to blame for all this— oh, not that I suggested her asking Stapleton to partner her—that was entirely her own idea. But I did suggest that if her father wouldn't let her work for Chalfont's, there was no reason why she shouldn't work for some other firm."

"I think that was a very sensible idea," Eleanor said matter-of-factly. "And there's no harm done, because Jervis told her that it was out of the question for her to work for them, but he's going to put her in touch with still another firm."

"Decent of him," Geoff said abstractedly. And then, rousing himself, "I didn't know you and he were on first name terms."

"We're not," Eleanor said quickly.

And that was true, of course. Yet this evening he had called her by her first name—and it had sounded extraordinarily natural—

She realised that Geoff was looking at her rather curiously and hastily consulted her programme.

"Oh, my goodness, my next dance is with Uncle Edgar," she exclaimed in dismay. "I simply can't dance with him—not after—" she stopped abruptly. Geoff, of course, didn't know what had happened in the rose garden after he had taken Celia away, and it was hardly fair to bother him with it. "And I'm quite sure he won't want to dance with me!"

"Well, cut him, and dance with Stapleton," Geoff said lazily. "That would properly put the cat among the pigeons!"

"Yes, it certainly would, wouldn't it!" Eleanor agreed with a not very mirthful laugh. "But no, if anyone's going to do any cutting, it's going to be Uncle Edgar, not me!"

But though she looked diligently for him, there was no sign of Edgar anywhere, and just as the band played the opening notes of the dance in question, she saw her Aunt Alice apparently just leaving the big house since she had a cloak over her shoulders.

"Oh, Aunt Alice, do you know where Uncle Edgar is?" she asked, and Alice turned to look at her with lacklustre eyes.

"Yes, he's gone home," she said in a flat voice. "He's —in one of his moods. I'm just going home as well in case there is anything I can do—"

Eleanor let her go without further comment, but for the first time she began to realise that if home life at the East Pavilion wasn't as pleasant as it might be, the fault might well lie with Edgar at least as much as with his wife, difficult though she could be.

With a little sigh, Eleanor turned away from the door deciding that it might be rather pleasant to go upstairs to her office and sit there quietly for a little while.

But as she reached the foot of the stairs, a tall figure obstructed her way.

"Are you, by any fortunate chance, disengaged for this dance?" Jervis asked hopefully. "Because if so, may I—?"

Eleanor's lips parted to tell him that she was too tired to dance, that some duty or other called her, but the words would not come, and as if in a dream, she found that she was dancing with Jervis, just as, jokingly, Geoff had suggested she should.

Then as, involuntarily, she surrendered to the charming lilt of an old-fashioned waltz, a strange thing happened. That she and Jervis were moving in perfect unison was no dream. It was reality. So real that everything else faded into unimportant obscurity—

Did Jervis feel the same thing? Perhaps he did, at

least for the moment, for his arm tightened round her and she heard him whisper her name in a way that asked a question and yet, surely, told her something as well.

Then the music stopped and the spell shattered to fragments though their hands still clung. Then their eyes met, and with a little gasp Eleanor tore herself free and fled away—somewhere—anywhere—so that she could hide her secret heart from him.

But, she wondered desperately, was there anywhere— any way in which she could hide it from herself?

*   *   *

The "do" had been on a Saturday. Two days later Eleanor began a drive to clear up any outstanding problems so that when she went on her honeymoon, she could do so with an easy conscience. It meant a good many interviews with departmental managers, a complete inspection with them in attendance of their particular section and the settling of several not too serious problems.

By the Wednesday, she felt confident that nothing untoward was likely to happen while she was away, at least, not as regards the employees and the pottery itself.

But Uncle Edgar? That was another matter entirely. Eleanor knew that she was still very much in his black books, as he avoided her whenever it was possible, and when they were compelled to meet, he was careful to keep from meeting her eyes. That, more than anything else, gave her the uneasy feeling that he had made or was making plans that he didn't want to give her a chance of even guessing, and so it would be quite useless to question him.

Naturally that didn't stop her from wondering, principally, of course, about that wonderful Jewel Series he had shown her. He had been so confident that he would be hearing from his agent in the very near future—"any day" was the phrase he had used. Well, no doubt there had to be a lot of very careful checking done before an application could be made and then, one knew that Government departments didn't move as quickly as one could sometimes wish, but all the same, as time went on.

she felt it was a little strange that he hadn't yet heard. Or that if he had, he'd said nothing to her. Surely, from the way he had spoken, he would have seized the first possible opportunity to emphasise the firm's dependence on his work?

Perhaps, she decided hopefully, he had realised that he was not in quite such a strong position as he had at first made out. Certainly she had done her best to make that clear, though at the time she had not been at all sure that she had succeeded. Well, time alone would show, but she could wish that the matter had come to a head before she went off on her honeymoon.

She was to have her wish. Early the next morning when she was still attending to her mail, Edgar burst into her room. He was clearly almost beside himself with anger, for his face was blotched and empurpled, and his eyes seemed to be starting out of his head. Incoherently he thrust a letter into Eleanor's hand and sank down into a chair, gasping for breath.

It was not a very long letter, but it was completely devastating. Edgar's agents had to inform him that after careful consideration, H. M. Patent Office regretted that it would be impossible to issue a patent to Mr. Edgar Chalfont covering the pottery process details which he had supplied as an all but identical process had already been patented by Messrs. Stapleton & Son of the Stapleton Potteries, Kingswell.

"But how incredible!" Eleanor exclaimed blankly. "I mean, a concidence like that—"

"Coincidence!" Edgar shouted. "Don't be a fool, girl! Somehow or other they've managed to get hold of my details and they've beaten me to it applying for a patent. Arrant theft, that's what it is, and by heavens, I'll get them for it if it's the last thing I do!" And he snatched the letter from her and made for the door, but Eleanor reached it first and stood with her back to it, barring his way.

"What are you going to do, Uncle?" she demanded.

"Do? Do?" He glared at her, red-eyed. "Go and tax them with it to their faces, of course—and don't try to stop me or you may get hurt!"

"You're not going out of this room until you've list-

ened to me," Eleanor said firmly, surprised that she
didn't feel in the least alarmed at his threat. "Do stop
to think for a minute! Is it possible for anyone to have
got at your private papers? Now is it?"

For a moment Edgar seemed to waver. Then his face
grew obstinate.

"They must have done," he insisted. "And don't ask
me how because naturally I don't know, but—"

"All right, let's just say that it would be very, very
difficult—is that true?"

"Yes," he admitted grudgingly.

"Very well, then," Eleanor said firmly. "If you go and
call them thieves, do you know what will happen?
They'll bring a case against you for slander—and one
of the things I'm pretty sure you'd have to prove would
be that at some time or other it has been reasonably
possible for someone to have seen your papers. Don't
you see—"

"I can see that, as usual, you're siding with that lot
against me," Edgar said viciously. "But neither you nor
they will get away with it this time! Do you think I'm
going to give in tamely to barefaced robbery—" he
choked on the words, pushed her out of the way and
was through the door in a flash. Eleanor heard his
footsteps hurrying down the corridor and raced after
him. She was rather hindered by her high heels, but
she caught him up in the car park, and wrenched open
the front passenger door.

"Of course I'm coming with you," she told him
breathlessly when he protested. "Do you think I'm going
to let you involve the firm without—"

"This isn't the firm's business, it's mine," he snarled.
"But come if you like. It may do you good to see that
young jackanapes having to grovel for once in his life!"

It wasn't a very long journey, but it was a nightmare
one. Edgar drove with a recklessness that earned him
several indignant hoots from other car drivers, and by
the time they reached the Stapleton potteries, Eleanor's
nerves were in tatters.

Edgar drew up with a jerk that shot Eleanor forward,
and while she was recovering her balance, he grabbed
the shabby old case which Eleanor remembered only

too well from the back seat of the car and dashed in through the main doors of the building. Eleanor followed as quickly as she could, but by the time she got inside, Edgar was already in trouble with the hall porter who, naturally, had stopped him to ask his business. Edgar, enraged at the check, was shouting at the top of his voice as Eleanor reached him.

"Now that won't do, sir," the man said, standing stolidly in Edgar's path. "You state your business properly and I'll see what I can do about it, but going on like this won't get you anywhere!" And then, as Edgar took no notice whatever, he turned appealingly to Eleanor. "Won't you please try to make him understand, miss, that I can't—"

But before Eleanor could speak, a door opened a short distance down the corridor and Jervis came out.

"What the devil's going on, Tompkins?" he demanded, and stopped short when he saw who the visitors were. Ignoring Edgar completely, he addressed Eleanor. "Something wrong? Anything I can do to help?"

"If you could spare just a few moments—" Eleanor suggested diffidently. "I think it would be the easiest and quickest way to clear things up—"

Jervis glanced fleetingly at Edgar.

"You're probably right," he agreed. "All right, Tompkins. You acted quite properly, but—" he left the sentence unfinished and led the way back to his room. Still ignoring Edgar, he pulled up a chair for Eleanor and sat down at his desk. "Now then?" he said crisply, though he smiled reassuringly at Eleanor.

Now completely beside himself as a result of the offhand treatment he had received, Edgar was almost dancing with rage. He shook a clenched fist in Jervis's face.

"You damned young thief—!" he shouted.

Without attempting to back away from the threatening fist Jervis stretched out his hand to the house telephone.

"If that's the sort of language you're going to indulge in, I'd like to have a witness present," he said coolly. "Oh, Father? Do you mind coming to my room for a minute? I've got a bit of trouble on hand—thanks!"

He replaced the telephone and stood up, pushing Edgar's fist away casually as he did so. "Just wait a moment, will you? My father's room is quite near. Proceedings will only be delayed a few moments. Ah, here he is!" as the door opened and Mr. Stapleton came in.

He looked surprised when he saw who his son's visitor's were and lifted his eyes enquiringly as he greeted Eleanor.

"Something wrong?" he asked her gravely.

"I'm afraid so—" Eleanor began, but Edgar interrupted her with an hysterically high-pitched laugh.

"Oh no, nothing wrong!" he said with heavy irony. "Simply you've stolen my process—" He set the case on the desk and fumbled with the lock. With shaking hands he took out the ruby cup and took off its wrappings. "There!" he said defiantly. "Now what have you got to say?"

The two Stapletons regarded the lovely thing attentively for several moments. Then Jervis turned questioningly to his father.

"I think so, don't you, Father?" he asked, and the old man nodded.

From his pocket Jervis drew a long, slim chain at the end of which were several keys. He selected one, and walking to the corner of the room, opened a small safe from which he took out a wooden box. He brought it back to his desk and opened it. From its nest of cotton wool he took out a cup and set it beside Edgar's.

Eleanor gave a little gasp. The two shapes varied slightly, but apart from that the two cups were identical —the same pale gold lining, the same rich, glowing colour set jewel-like in a slender tracery of gold—

Edgar, after staring unbelievingly at the two cups, cackled scornfully.

"And you've got the nerve to pretend it's all your own idea!" he scoffed. "Why, anyone with half an eye can see—why, you haven't got a leg to stand on!"

"Mr. Chalfont, please control yourself," Jervis said coldly. "It is, I agree, an amazing coincidence—"

"Coincidence!" Edgar gave that cackling laugh again. "Barefaced robbery!"

Tight-lipped, Jervis turned to Eleanor.

"Miss Chalfont, this is a very surprising and unfortunate state of affairs, but abuse will get us nowhere! If you will be so good—"

"That'll do, young man," Edgar interrupted. "No doubt you'd prefer to deal with an inexperienced girl whose head you can hope to turn, but this is *my* affair, not the firm's. You deal with me!"

Jervis looked questioningly at Eleanor, who nodded.

"All my uncle's designs are his own personal copyright," she acknowledged tonelessly, and saw Jervis's eyes narrow.

"Indeed? A peculiar arrangement! However—" he turned to Edgar—"if you wish, we'll postpone this discussion until your solicitor and ours can be present. Or, if you are willing to answer one question, we may be able to settle it without going to that length. Well?"

A muscle twitched nervously at the corner of Edgar's mouth.

"What's the question?" he asked suspiciously.

"Simply this—when did you first work out this process? I don't mean in its final form, but the initial idea?"

For a moment Eleanor held her breath, convinced that her uncle would never give an answer, but to her surprise he said almost triumphantly:

"Almost a year ago!" as if it was his crowning arguement.

Jervis accepted the statement without question, but what he did say was infinitely more devastating to Edgar's claim than any argument could be.

"And has your agent not told you that we took out our patent for the perfected process twenty months ago?"

"What!" Edgar shouted incredulously. "I don't believe it—" he fumbled in his pocket for the letter he had shown Eleanor and opened it with shaking hands. Then Eleanor saw his jaw drop and the colour fade from his face. Her hands tightened their grasp on the chair arms.

"So he did tell you," Jervis said positively, and indeed, no one could help but draw that inference. "You see what this means, Mr. Chalfont? This is a coincidence based, I imagine, on the fact that the ingredient used to obtain this effect is comparatively new and there is no secret about it. It was inevitable that its application to pottery should occur to more than one person—a pity, no doubt, but these things do happen, you know—"

"I don't believe it," Edgar muttered through dry lips. "Somehow, you're tricking me—"

"Mr. Chalfont, you're talking nonsense." For the first time the older Stapleton intervened, his voice measured and stern. "You have confirmation that we were first in the field from an independent source—and one, moreover, whom you presumably trust since he is your agent. We perfected our process before the possibility of such a thing even occurred to you. Of what use then would your details be to us? We're not interested in them because we'd worked it all out for ourselves long before! Oh no, no suspicion can be attached to us, however difficult you may find it to believe. But can the same be said about *you*?"

"Oh no, *no*!" Eleanor said in a horrified whisper, and involuntarily, it seemed, Jervis was drawn to her chair to stand behind her, his hands resting lightly on her shoulders, though, as with her, his eyes never left Edgar's face.

And, as the significance of what Mr. Stapleton had said sank in, Edgar seemed to shrink and shrivel as he had done that other time in the rose garden. He knew he was beaten—and he was frightened because, at last, he had realised what an equivocal position he was in. His eyes wandered to each of the three faces in turn. Then they dropped.

"I didn't—" he began, and stopped as if he knew no denial of his would carry any weight. "You've no—" and stopped once again.

Then, suddenly, his nerve gave completely. He put his head down and dashed from the room, slamming the door behind him.

Instantly Eleanor jumped to her feet.

"Please, please stop him!" she begged frantically. "He isn't fit to drive—"

The same realisation had come to both the Stapleton men. Jervis wrenched open the door and dashed after

Edgar while Mr. Stapleton lifted the house phone.

"Main gate lodge—urgently!" he said imperatively, and then: "What? But he must be there! Try again—no, don't worry," and hung up.

For it was too late. A shattering crash, people shouting—

And then a silence that was worst of all.

CHAPTER X

EDGAR had been killed outright.

Blindly reckless—or perhaps indifferent to danger—he had driven straight out of the big gates into the busy road without taking even minimal care at the very moment when a heavy oil tanker was passing. As the shaken gatekeeper said, he hadn't had a chance.

Eleanor, stunned by what had happened, was persuaded to stay in Jervis's office while he and his father made sure that the necessary machinery for summoning an ambulance and the police had been set in motion.

As soon as she was alone, Eleanor buried her face in her hands, trying desperately to pull herself together, but for the time being, it was beyond her power to think coherently. It was not that she had a feeling of personal loss because Edgar Chalfont had never been the sort of man who attracted affection, but the circumstances of his death were such that even a stranger would have been horrified—and when all was said and done, he was Eleanor's kith and kin. Deep, tearless sobs shook her and she shivered as if it was a bleak winter day instead of a glorious golden August one.

The door must have been opened to admit someone, for she heard the slight chink as a tray was set down on the desk. She looked up quickly and saw that it was Jervis. He brought a steaming cup over to her.

"I want you to drink this coffee," he said quietly.

"You see, the police will need to ask you some questions, and I think this may help—"

"Yes—thank you," Eleanor said shakily, but before she began to drink, she asked the question that had been haunting her. "Jervis, do you think he knew much—" No, she couldn't finish it.

Jervis laid his hand over her free one and held it tightly.

"I truly believe it must have been so quick that he knew little or nothing—" Jervis assured her with convincing sincerity, and Eleanor gave a quick little sigh of relief.

"I'm glad of that—so glad," she told him. "All the more so because everything has been so difficult—" she bit her lip. "Jervis, do you really think he stole your idea —the new process, I mean?"

"No, I don't," Jervis said unhesitatingly. "For one thing, I don't think he'd have been such a fool as to imagine he'd get away with it. For another, his mental distress over this wasn't acting. It was terribly genuine. And, finally, I'm satisfied that our security arrangements were sufficiently good for it to have been impossible for the secret to have leaked out. No, it was coincidence, I'm sure of that. But it's one I'd have given my right hand for it not to be our firm which was concerned. You do believe that, Eleanor?"

"Yes, I do," she said slowly. "Just as I believe that your father only suggested that suspicion could have been attached to Uncle Edgar in a last-hope effort to bring him to his senses."

"That was it," Jervis was clearly relieved that she had said that. "But it doesn't stop Father feeling terribly troubled because he did say it. He feels that if he hadn't, this might not have happened—"

"It might not have done," Eleanor admitted. "But I'm not too sure. Uncle Edgar wasn't in a condition to drive in any case—I know that, because we almost crashed coming here." She shivered at the memory. "It was a nightmare! It was only sheer luck and other people's good driving that saved us!"

"If anything had happened to you—" Jervis began impetuously, and stopped short because the door opened and his father came in followed by an Inspector of Police.

Eleanor and he knew each other slightly, and he was as considerate as was possible, but even so, when the interview was over, Eleanor felt that she was at the end of her tether. And yet, she knew, the worst was yet to come—Aunt Alice had to be told what had happened, and it was Eleanor's job to do it. There could be no doubt about that.

So, when the Inspector had asked all his questions and had explained that there would have to be an inquest which she would be required to attend, she asked Jervis if he would ring up her office to explain what had happened and to ask that her car should be brought over by someone who could then drive her home.

"Because I don't think I can drive myself—" she confessed, biting her lip.

"It would be foolish to try," Jervis assured her understandingly. "But I can think of a better arrangement. Father will ring through to explain what has happened, and I'll drive you home. We can see about your car later. Now, if you agree?"

It couldn't be put off, Eleanor knew, so though she was not too sure that it was altogether a good plan, she did not waste time arguing. It was only when they were on their way that she realised just how thoughtful Jervis had been. Had one of her own employees been driving it would have been necessary to explain and possibly discuss the accident. More questions—it would have been unbearable! As it was, she could just sit quietly beside Jervis—

But as they neared Kingsworthy House, she was reminded of an earlier occasion when he had driven her home.

"It's strange, isn't it, that whenever I'm concerned in a family emergency, it's you who come to my rescue," she said involuntarily.

Jervis gave her a brief, penetrating look as if he wasn't quite sure just how she meant that. And it might have been that Eleanor herself didn't really know either, yet he seemed to be satisfied.

"I truly regret the emergencies," he said quietly. "But

I'm genuinely glad if I've been able to help you at all."

There was a questioning inflection in his voice, and Eleanor acted and spoke with an impulsiveness which surprised her. Laying her hand on his arm, she said emphatically:

"You have helped—tremendously. I—I don't know what I'd have done without you on either occasion."

There was the briefest of pauses before he replied:

"I'm glad!" And was silent until, turning in at the gates of Kingsworthy house, he asked: "Straight to the East Pavilion?"

Eleanor drew a deep breath.

"Yes, please." And she wished she could ask him to come in with her to break the news to Aunt Alice, but that would be taking too great an advantage of his helpfulness.

But she need not have worried. When they reached the East Pavilion, it was clear that he had no intention of leaving her to face up to the situation on her own, as his reassuring smile made clear.

"Of course I'm coming with you—unless you'd rather I didn't?"

"I'll be thankful—" Eleanor began, and stopped short.

Laughing and talking together, their hands linked, Geoff and Celia had suddenly appeared round the corner of the Pavilion. They stopped dead when they saw who was standing there. Then Celia darted forward.

"Something's the matter, isn't it?" she gasped. "You wouldn't be here at this time of day if it wasn't—and I can see it in your face, Eleanor! What is it? You've got to tell me!" In her agitation she caught hold of Eleanor's arm and shook it violently. "It's Father, isn't it? Something's happened to Father!"

Eleanor moistened her lips with the tip of her tongue.

"Yes," she said heavily. "There—there's been an accident, Celia—"

Celia's eyes widened in horror.

"You mean—he's dying—no, he's dead, isn't he?" Her voice rose hysterically. "That's what you mean, isn't it?"

"Yes, darling," Eleanor said reluctantly, and tried to put her arms round her young cousin. But Celia, tears streaming down her face, pushed her away, and turning, fled back to Geoff.

"Geoff, Geoff—" she moaned, and held out her arms to him.

To Eleanor, watching, it seemed as if nothing was quite real any more, as if this was a dream—

For, as Geoff took Celia in his arms, his eyes met Eleanor's and in them she read both shame—and a great tenderness. But the tenderness was not for her.

"Shall we go in?" Jervis asked quietly, and with a start, Eleanor turned her back on the two figures locked in one another's arms. By and by she would have to do something about them, but for the present, there was a more pressing duty—

There was no sign of hysteria in Alice Chalfont's reception of the news. No emotion of any sort. Simply, she seemed to freeze. Only when both Eleanor and Jervis asked her if there was anything they could do did she show any feeling at all. And then it was simply impatience.

"No, nothing at all, thank you," she said brusquely. "I am perfectly competent to do whatever is necessary."

"Yes, of course," Eleanor murmured uncomfortably. "I thought perhaps you might like me to ring up Mr. Franklin—"

"Thank you, no. I propose doing that myself at once," Alice replied, and seeing that their presence was obviously unwelcome, Eleanor and Jervis left her, already looking up her list of telephone numbers.

"I don't feel really happy about leaving her," Eleanor said uncertainly. "Do you think she'll be all right?"

"I should think so," Jervis said without, it would seem, very much interest. "In any case, I don't see what you could do for her because she obviously preferred to be alone. Some people do on these occasions. I think I would myself. But now, what about you? What do you propose doing?"

"I—" Eleanor glanced down at her watch and was surprised to see how early it still was. How incredible that so much could have happened in so short a time! Unconsciously she looked round, but there was no sign of either Celia or Geoff. "I don't think there's anything for me to do here, and in any case, I really ought to go back to the works. Even if Aunt Alice is going to get in touch with Mr. Franklin, I shall have to as well—" she paused, appalled at the realisation of all the new problems and complications her uncle's death would almost certainly cause.

"Yes, I think that's your obvious first move," Jervis agreed matter-of-factly. "Particularly as, since your aunt's attitude is what it is, he'll make a useful liaison between you. How about letting Miss Chalfont know? Would you like to call in on her before returning to Kingswell?"

"It's no use doing that—she won't be there," Eleanor explained. "She's up in town at her flat until Friday." And remembered with a pang just why Aunt Helen was returning then. It was in order to be able to give her away at her wedding the next day. Only now there wouldn't be a wedding. She knew that beyond doubt, and the reason was only indirectly due to her uncle's death. That, it was true, had sent Celia flying to Geoff's arms for comfort which in itself had aroused in him a tenderness that was unmistakably akin to love. So there was only one thing to do—give Geoff his freedom without recrimination of any sort. But not just immediately. She must have a little time to herself before she faced up to the inevitable interview.

"Then shall we get going?" Jervis asked.

Eleanor, roused from her thoughts with a little start, apologised for having delayed him.

"And, in fact, for having taken up so much of your time," she went on. "Particularly after—after the way Uncle Edgar—" the words choked in her throat as she remembered that appalling scene in Jervis's office.

Rather to her surprise, Jervis answered her almost impatiently.

"Look, Eleanor, you mustn't let yourself dwell on that! For one thing, the poor devil was beside himself with disappointment. And in any case, you didn't come with him to give him your backing, did you? My impression was that you hoped to be able to prevent trouble."

"Yes," Eleanor sighed, "that was it. But I didn't have much success, did I?"

"I don't think anybody would have done," Jervis replied thoughtfully. "He was beyond reason—"

They fell silent for the rest of the journey, but when they reached the works and Eleanor was getting out, Jervis said quietly:

"I shall be getting in touch with you in order to let you have documented proof of our claim to have been well ahead with this new process."

"Oh!" Eleanor said blankly. "But I do believe you, you know."

Jervis smiled for the first time since they had met that morning.

"For that I'm really thankful," he told her. "And grateful to you for having told me. All the same, this doesn't only concern you, does it?"

"I don't think I—" she began, puzzled by his remark.

"But, my dear," he said with a certain surprise, "of course, I don't know the terms of your partnership agreement, but don't you see that whoever inherits your uncle's share is very likely to want satisfaction on that point?"

"Yes," Eleanor wondered how she could have failed to see that for herself. "Particularly if it's Aunt Alice."

"Exactly," Jervis agreed. "So, as I said, I'll let you have all the details—or would you rather I sent them to Franklin?"

"Yes," Eleanor said after a moment's thought. "That would be the best thing. I'll just give him an outline of what happened, and then he'll be in the picture. Good-bye—and thank you again."

Jervis smiled, lifted his hand in salute and drove away. Eleanor took a deep breath and went in through the big swing doors to face up to all that awaited her.

*   *   *

It was late that evening before Eleanor reached home after a day she would never forget.

From the moment when, after leaving Jervis, she had entered the works, she had been sensitive to a queer subdued excitement all around her that put her in mind

of the agitated hum from a beehive just before a swarm.
People were talking about what had happened, or if
they weren't talking, then thinking, so that the air was
tense with speculation and, she thought, even apprehension.

However, except for the receptionist and the hall
porter, she encountered no one on her way to her room,
and realised gratefully that this was evidence of real
consideration. But of course, she could only put off seeing her senior employees for a short time. Just while
she made two telephone calls, in fact.

The first call was to Mr. Franklin who, having briefly
expressed his regrets for what had happened, told her
that he had already heard the news from Alice Chalfont.

"I am, in fact, about to leave for Kingsworthy House,"
he explained. "Mrs. Chalfont wishes to discuss the various arrangements that must be made with me—"

"Yes, of course," Eleanor said quickly, thinking that
there had been a slightly uncertain note in his voice as
if he thought Eleanor might feel he had in some way
intruded. "I knew she intended ringing you up."

"I shall, of course, also need to see you," Mr. Franklin
went on. "If it's convenient for me to call when I return
to Kingswell—say about two-thirty?"

"Yes, I shall be in all afternoon."

When he had rung off, she got through to Helen
Chalfont, who immediately announced her intention of
leaving for home immediately.

"And I'll come and see you this evening," she promised, and then, in consternation: "Child, what about
your wedding?"

"There won't be any wedding," Eleanor said quietly,
and rang off before Helen could say any more.

Then the departmental heads had to be summoned.
A discreet explanation of what had happened without
making any reference to the cause of Edgar's mental
distress. That, the police had felt, should not be made
public in the meantime. The question might be asked
at the inquest and would then, of course, have to be
answered, but until then—

When that was over, a representative of the local

newspaper had to be seen. He was frankly curious since the rivalry between the two firms was public knowledge. When, then, had the two of them gone over to Stapleton's?

"On business," Eleanor explained briefly.

"Anything to do with the merger that's been—rather more than hinted at?" the reporter asked, surveying her shrewdly.

"Nothing whatever," Eleanor said steadily. The house telephone rang and she answered it, hoping that whatever the message was, it would provide her with an excuse to get rid of this persistent and thick-skinned young man. It did. "And now I must ask you to go because my solicitor is here and, as you can no doubt imagine, we have quite a lot to discuss. Good afternoon!"

The young man went, and a few moments later Mr. Franklin was shown in. He looked considerably harassed and years older than he really was. After one look at him, Eleanor lifted the telephone and ordered tea for them both.

"I shall be glad of that," he said gratefully, wiping his forehead with his handkerchief. "Quite frankly, I can't remember ever having such a distressing interview—" he shook his head and sighed deeply. "I knew that there was some feeling on Mrs. Chalfont's part—but I had no idea it went so deep or was so intransigent! Ough!" He blew his nose ferociously. "Well, there's no need for you to be bothered with the details—though I had to be—but the long and the short of it is that Mrs. Edgar fervently hates Chalfont's and everything to do with them! As she put it, nothing but unhappiness had come to her since becoming a member of the family, and she'd endured it all for the sake of the children. Now that was a thing of the past and she intended leaving Kingsworthy House—and, for that matter, Kingswell, and returning to her own people."

"I see," Eleanor paused as the tray of tea was brought in by one of the messenger girls, and set on the desk. Eleanor poured out the two cups of tea before she spoke again. "Perhaps she had cause to feel like that—"

"I think she had, my dear." He sipped the tea gratefully. "I don't think Edgar could ever have been an easy man to live with—it always seemed to me that he had two personalities. For a long time I was not at all sure which was the more genuine—they were certainly contradictory. But recently I've had less doubt and, frankly, I've been worried—" he cocked an enquiring eye at her.

"I know. So have I," Eleanor agreed. "Not that I realised it until very recently. But do you think he *really* had two personalities? I think that the one most people knew, the quiet recessive type, was—oh, it doesn't sound very kind, but I think it was deliberately assumed at least to some degree—"

"H'm!" Mr. Franklin pondered. "Yes, you may be right. And when did you realise—?"

"Looking back, I think it was shortly after Uncle Simon died," Eleanor told him. "Yes, I'm sure it was, although I didn't appreciate the significance of some of the things he said until later. But this morning—" she bit her lip as the horror of what had happened returned vividly to her mind.

"Yes, you'd better tell me just exactly what happened," Mr. Franklin suggested. "I gather he was worked up over something—but so far I don't know what it was. You didn't go into details to Mrs. Chalfont either?"

"No, I didn't," Eleanor admitted. "I rather felt as if I ought to, but she didn't ask any questions, and the police felt that until after the inquest, the fewer people who knew just why it had happened, the better. But she'll have to know, of course—"

"And so shall I," Mr. Franklin said firmly. "And the sooner the better!"

So Eleanor told him exactly what had happened, doing her best to be strictly factual, but when she came to the end of her story, her voice shook as she recalled that appalling crash—

"An extremely nasty experience for you," Mr. Franklin said sympathetically. "And one which I'm afraid will have repercussions. Now, did the Stapletons produce any *proof* of their story that they were well ahead of your uncle with this process?"

"No, they didn't. But then Uncle Edgar's agent told him that in the letter that came this morning. Only Uncle was so—so shattered by the news that he didn't read as far as that until he got to the Stapletons'. That was just before he dashed out— All the same, Jervis Stapleton said he'd let me have details of their patent—or rather, we decided it had better come to you."

"Excellent!" Mr. Franklin approved, and hesitated. For a moment he drummed his fingers irritably on the desk then, explosively, he said : "I don't know when I've been in such an awkward position—never, in fact! You realise, of course, that as well as being the firm's solicitor, I have also always handled the private affairs of both your uncles—and Mrs. Chalfont wishes me to look after hers. And frankly, I don't know if it's honestly possible to do that!"

"You mean, Aunt Alice is being difficult?" Eleanor suggested uncertainly.

"Difficult!" Mr. Franklin gave a laugh that was really a snort. "Well, I suppose you could call it that. But not in any positive sort of way. It's more that—I suppose you know your uncle left his share in the firm to his wife?"

"No, I didn't," Eleanor admitted, conscious of an unpleasant sense of chill. "But I suppose it was only natural—"

"Possibly, possibly," Mr. Franklin said testily. "Though personally, I don't approve of a partnership deed being so loosely worded that the most unsuitable people—however, it's too late to do anything about that, though, believe me, I tried when it was drawn up. The point is this—I'm convinced that Mrs. Chalfont didn't know the terms of her husband's will, either. When I told her, something happened—until then, her face had been utterly expressionless—"

"Frozen?" Eleanor suggested quickly, and the solicitor nodded.

"Exactly! But then there was a change. I wouldn't say that the information gave her *pleasure*. But intense satisfaction, yes. As if she realised—" he broke off, shaking his head.

"As if she realised the power it gave her—and knew

exactly what use she would make of it?" Eleanor suggested.

"Yes, just that," Mr. Franklin conceded. "And you see in what an impossible position it puts me! Both you and she are my clients, and as such, I owe loyalty to both of you. But if those loyalties clash—"

"As I think they could," Eleanor said quietly. "I remember Celia telling me that her mother regarded Chalfont's as a sort of greedy, grasping monster, and what she said to you today confirms that—"

"Well, as I see it, the situation is this—I am willing to act for Mrs. Chalfont in making the necessary arrangements for the funeral and in obtaining probate of her husband's will. But not anything more than that —and so I told her."

"Did she mind?" Eleanor asked quickly.

"Apparently not. She simply nodded as if she wasn't really surprised. I don't like it—I'm most uneasy—"

They were both silent for a time and then Eleanor said tentatively :

"Don't you think it's possible that appreciating that it's a situation I can't be expected to like, Aunt Alice has made up her mind to sell out her share, but at a greatly enhanced price?"

"Yes, it could be that," Mr. Franklin agreed heavily. "Well, there it is. You can't make a person tell you what's in their mind—so all we can do is wait until Mrs. Chalfont makes a move."

Again they were silent and then, in a different voice, Mr. Franklin asked Eleanor what she intended doing about her wedding.

"My own opinion is that since it was to be such a very quiet family affair, you should not consider cancelling the arrangement—"

Eleanor swallowed the lump that suddenly came into her throat.

"There—won't be a wedding," she said curtly. "Not because of Uncle Edgar, but because we've both decided—" and could say no more.

"But, my dear—" Mr. Franklin's eyes fell to Geoff's ring that she was still wearing, "surely there must be some mistake—"

Eleanor snatched off the ring and dropped it into her pocket.

"So much else has happened that I forgot—" she explained, feeling, as she spoke, how unconvincing that was.

"Yes, of course, I see," Mr. Franklin accepted the explanation with apparent equanimity. He stood up. "Well, I think that's all for the moment. You will keep in touch with me if—if there are any developments?"

"I will," Eleanor promised, and shook hands before seeing him to the door.

*　　*　　*

Helen Chalfont reached the West Pavilion only a few minutes after Eleanor reached home. As soon as she realised the situation, she suggested going home and either coming back later or else leaving it until the following day for a talk.

"No, stay, please, Aunt Helen," Eleanor said restlessly. "I must talk to someone."

Helen Chalfont made no comment other than to ask Eleanor when she had last had anything to eat.

"I don't know—breakfast, I think," Eleanor confessed.

"In that case, no wonder you look as if you're going into a decline," Helen said critically. "Come along and we'll ransack your pantry!"

"I don't really feel like eating," Eleanor demurred, but her aunt took no notice.

"Soup first," she decided, and opened a can into a saucepan. "After that, we'll see how you feel."

Once she had drunk the hot soup, Eleanor found that she had more of an appetite than she had realised, and when half an hour later the two of them sat down with their coffees, Eleanor confessed that she felt considerably better.

"Of course you do, my dear," Helen said cheerfully. "And now tell me all about it."

And so once again Eleanor had to tell the whole distressing story, right up to when she had said goodbye to Mr. Franklin.

"It's odd," Helen reflected as she helped herself to more coffee, "the way in which the two firms—or perhaps I should say the two families—have for so many years been concerned in each other's affairs. Of course, right from the beginning, when Stapleton's first started up, there was a certain amount of feeling on Grandfather's part. But it only showed itself in a sort of healthy, normal rivalry. It was only later that it developed into—"

"Vicious rivalry?" Eleanor suggested, remembering that Jervis had used those words and deplored the existence of such a feeling.

"Yes, just that," Helen agreed. "And of course, Edgar was at the bottom of it. All his life he's made trouble, you know. Never openly until, it would appear, just recently. But somehow he's always contrived to influence other people so that he got his own way. What you have told me about him saying so apologetically that his personal feeling was for Chalfont's to continue on their own was typical. He made you feel that you weren't being fair to him, particularly as he had promised you his loyalty, if you didn't take his feelings into consideration."

"Yes, that's perfectly true," Eleanor agreed. "I hadn't thought of it that way, but you're quite right."

"Oh yes, I'm quite right," Helen said sadly. "He was a very dangerous man, Eleanor. Far more dangerous than either Father or Simon. Granted they liked to have their own way—but they were honest about it—there was none of this mendacity that Edgar had. He always preferred to work in the background with someone else as his cat's-paw. I suppose you realise that it was Edgar who let the cat out of the bag over that possible merger?"

"Yes. I didn't see who else it could be," Eleanor replied. "But why, Aunt Helen? That's what I want to know! Why did he hate Stapleton's so bitterly?"

"Why? Oh, my dear, that's only too simple," Helen said with a sigh. "He fell in love with a girl, and she turned him down in favour of—Jervis's father. He could never forget or forgive that—even though, later on, he married Alice, poor soul."

"I see," Eleanor drew a deep breath. "Yes, that explains a lot."

"It certainly explains why he saw to it that I didn't marry Lucas Stapleton—did you know about that?"

"Jervis told me. He said you might have been his aunt as well as mine—"

"Yes, so I might!" Helen agreed. "I expect he told you the circumstances—how short a time we'd known one another before deciding to get married? Well, I believed, for a long time that, mistaken though I believed them to be, at least they were convinced that they had my well-being at heart. Years later, I found out the truth. At first I couldn't believe it, but then I had irrefutable proof," her face twisted with pain. "It came to me in a roundabout way, but when I challenged Edgar—our parents were dead by then—he admitted that it was he who had influenced them by telling them scurrilous and entirely untrue stories about Lucas. As a result, I've been a lonely woman all my life. Oh, I know, Lucas was killed, so I'd have been a widow, but at least we'd have had some happiness together—and there might have been a baby—and now," briskly, "that's enough about the past. It's over now—and the sooner we can all put it behind us the better. What I want to know, Eleanor, is just what you meant when you told me over the phone that there won't be any wedding? You've decided to postpone it?"

"No, Aunt Helen," Eleanor said steadily. "As far as Geoff and I are concerned, there won't ever be any wedding. We've realised it would be a mistake."

Helen looked shrewdly at her niece.

"I'm not going to ask you what's made you come to that conclusion," she said gravely, "because that's no one's business but your own. All I'm going to ask is—are you perfectly certain in your own mind that it's the right thing to do? It isn't, for example, any question of injured pride? Because if it is, believe me, my dear, where love's concerned, pride isn't worth a ha'penny!"

"No, I don't think it is," Eleanor agreed. "But pride doesn't come into this—except that Geoff doesn't need to ask for his freedom. I'm giving it to him."

"I see," Helen said, and wondered if Eleanor realised just how much she had revealed the true state of affairs. But she had no intention of asking that either.

A little later she left, and shortly after Geoff came over. Eleanor had only one desire—to get what must be a painful interview for both of them over as quickly as possible. So, before he could say anything, she told him quietly that she quite understood. He had made a mistake in thinking he loved her—and here was his ring.

Shamefacedly Geoff took it from her, and reproached himself bitterly for having let her down. Yet he could not refrain from trying to excuse his behaviour.

"I did tell you that I knew myself for the sort of chap who doesn't really grow up until he's got a wife and children depending on him. And Celia does depend on me. She *needs* me in a way—forgive me, Eleanor, but I think it's the truth, that you never did."

"Perhaps not," Eleanor conceded. "But it's not worth trying to work out the whys and wherefores. It's happened, and perhaps it's just as well, because I've realised, for a woman, business and marriage don't work."

"I think you're probably right," Geoff said slowly. "At least for yourself, because at heart you always have been a career woman, haven't you?"

She couldn't find the words to answer him, but she managed to smile, and to her relief, he took that as meaning that she agreed with him.

When he had gone she sat very still for a long time, staring unseeingly in front of her, not capable even of thinking.

It was some time before she realised that she wasn't *feeling* anything either.

No sense of loss, no heartbreak, no resentment.

Just—utter emptiness.

*   *   *

Eleanor got through the next week or so with a sort of mechanical precision that enabled her to do all that had to be done with no feeling of being personally involved.

Even when on the morning of the day she was to have been married a cable of congratulations and good wishes came from her mother, her only reaction was to think how perfectly dreadful her mother would feel about the *faux pas* which she had committed when she received the letter telling her all that had happened.

Much of that day Eleanor spent in her car driving rather aimlessly along minor roads through villages whose names she could never afterwards remember.

When, quite late that night, she returned to Kingsworthy House, she was so sleepy with all the fresh air and sunshine that, yawning her head off, she went to bed at once. She did remember, as she was dropping off to sleep, however, that she and Geoff had planned to spend this evening at the theatre, and her last conscious thought was an eminently practical one. Had Geoff remembered to return the tickets? It would be a pity if their two seats remained unoccupied, as it was an extremely popular show, and tickets were not easy to come by.

*   *   *

The inquest was held early the next week. Acting on Mr. Franklin's advice, Eleanor answered the questions she was asked as simply as possible, volunteering no additional information. So, when asked how Edgar had driven on their way to Stapleton's, she had said, with complete truth, that his driving had been very erratic and yes, she had been frightened.

Alice, rather to Eleanor's surprise since she now knew all the details of that fateful morning, contented herself with saying, in a completely toneless voice, that her husband's nerves had been greatly shaken by his brother's recent death. It did not particularly surprise her that the accident had occurred. He was too highly strung to make a good driver.

And that was really all. No one seemed to think it relevant to ask just why Edgar had been particularly worked up that morning, the tanker driver was exonerated from all blame and a verdict of accidental death recorded.

The following day Edgar was buried. Apart from the immediate family only Mr. Franklin was present, and after the short graveside ceremony, Alice showed no signs whatever of wanting to speak either to Eleanor or Helen. Nor did they feel, in the face of such evident hostility, that they would make any advance to her.

"And I think that's how it's going to be," Helen remarked to Eleanor as they went back to the West Pavilion. "She will cut herself off entirely from both of us—and perhaps that's the best thing for everybody concerned. I suppose you're going back to work?"

"Yes, I must. There's so much to be done. We hadn't got everything settled up after Uncle Simon died. Now this—" Eleanor sighed. "I do wish I knew what Aunt Alice intends doing about her share in the firm."

"Probably you'll hear now that the funeral is over," Helen suggested. "I expect Mr. Franklin will have something to tell you soon." ·

But when Mr. Franklin spoke to Eleanor on the telephone the next day, he could tell her nothing, although he had gone so far as to tell Alice point blank that she must say what she intended doing with as little delay as possible. Her answer to that had simply been that she was considering the matter, and refused to discuss it further.

Two days later, however, just before leaving home in the morning, Eleanor received two letters. One was from her mother and she read that first. After having referred in a shocked way to Edgar's death, Kitty touched with tactful briefness on Eleanor's broken engagement, and went on :

"Cranmer and I plan to get married as soon as we can after reaching London in about ten days' time. Now, darling, seeing that Edgar's no longer able to be obstructive, and Alice, if I know her, will sell out to you if you offer her enough, why don't you let Stapleton's have their take-over, the way they wanted it? Then you could come to America with us—now don't say 'No' without giving it a thought, because it's just as much Cranmer's idea as it is mine!"

Eleanor laid the letter down with a little sigh. To start a new life in a new country—how marvellous that would be! But it wasn't quite as simple as that. Stapleton's might no longer be interested, for one thing.

She picked up the other letter without much interest. It bore a local postmark, but the writing was unfamiliar. Then she opened it and her eyes widened. It was a personally written letter from Jervis Stapleton, but it was brief and very businesslike.

"We have received a letter from Mrs. Alice Chalfont," he wrote, "in which she offers us the shares in your firm which were left to her by her late husband.

"Before giving an answer either way, we feel very strongly that we must discuss such a transaction with you.

"May I, as representing our firm, call and see you at either your office or your home? Perhaps you will let me know which you would prefer, and will suggest a time convenient to you?"

CHAPTER XI

SO that was how Alice Chalfont proposed paying off her score! Knowing the rivalry, and in Edgar's case the actual hatred that existed between the two families, she had deliberately sought to give the Stapletons the power to be at least a thorn in the surviving Chalfonts' flesh, as she undoubtedly hoped they would be. The terms of the letter which she had written and which Jervis showed to Eleanor left no doubt as to that.

"Though, for the life of me, I can't see why she should have her knife in *you*," Jervis remarked as she handed the letter back.

Knowing that Alice had already gone with Celia to her old home in Sussex, Eleanor had asked Jervis to come to Kingsworthy House, and because the weather had broken and the air was chilly and raw, they sat on either side of the hearth in which a wood fire gently burned. "Simon and Edgar—yes. I think she had got a grouch there, but you—that's different."

"I don't think it is," Eleanor disagreed. "I think I was, to her mind, just the last straw. You see, Uncle Edgar didn't feel he had a square deal when his father died and he got such a small share in the family firm.

Then, when Uncle Simon died, he was passed over in my favour. I think having to accept me, a girl, and his niece at that, as the senior partner must have infuriated him. In fact I know it did. He simply couldn't accept it. That was why he—why he was so desperately upset when he found that he couldn't use his Jewel Series as a—a bartering point with me."

"Yes, I wondered if it was something like that," Jervis admitted. "And so you mean she blames you for what happened—"

"Oh, more than that, I think," Eleanor said wearily. "I think she believes I had an opportunity of influencing Uncle Simon to pass Uncle Edgar over in my favour— and that was really the cause of his being so difficult. And I think she may have been right except that if it's true I had that opportunity, I certainly didn't make use of it. I had no idea what Uncle Simon had done— and I wish to goodness he never had." And her voice shook with the fervour of that wish.

"In that case—" Jervis began, stopped and started again. "Look, Eleanor, it's no good beating about the bush. I'm convinced—and so is Father—that Mrs. Chalfont intends to make as much difficulty for you as possible. She wrote to us first because, I suppose, we were the obvious market. But if we turn down her offer, she still won't sell out to you if she can possibly avoid it. She'll do her utmost to sell to some other firm. Of course, it's only fair to you to point out that she may not be able to find any purchasers in which case she would, I suppose, be driven to coming to you. But I doubt if you could gamble on it."

"No," Eleanor said slowly, "I don't think I could. I'm not sure I want to."

He looked at her sharply, but waited in silence for her to say more.

"It's very terrible, isn't it, that a man's death should set so many people free," she said musingly. "Aunt Alice is going to live with her people. They're farmers and I expect that eventually, Richard will learn farming from them. It's what he's always wanted to do. Celia—" unconsciously she held her head a little higher—"will marry Geoff—"

Still Jervis did not speak.

"And I," she went on after a moment's pause, "am free to get rid of a burden I never wanted—and want now, less than ever."

"I think I'll have to ask you to explain just what that means," Jervis said quietly. "I don't want to jump to the wrong conclusion—"

Eleanor leaned forward to put another log on the fire.

"Oh, it's perfectly simple," she told him matter-of-factly. "I'll raise no objection whatever to you accepting Aunt Alice's offer, but on one condition—"

"Yes?"

As she sat back in her chair she saw that his hands had tightened over the arms of his chair.

"It's quite a straightforward one," she explained. "You will have to buy me out as well. Do you understand? It won't be a merger or a partnership. It will be a complete take-over. Well?"

Jervis drew a breath so deep that it was almost a sigh.

"You understand that I shall have to discuss this with my father?" he asked, and she nodded.

"Oh yes, of course. But do you think he's likely to object? After all, it is what you've really wanted all along, isn't it? I mean, you remember you said, very early on, that a merger would never work—or rather that we would never be able to work together. Don't you remember?"

"Yes, I do," Jervis said slowly. "But I may have been mistaken—"

"No, I don't think you were. We're both too self-opinionated to be business partners."

"Maybe—though I've sometimes thought we might have been good friends, if things had been different."

"Yes, perhaps we might," she agreed. "But as you say, if things had been different. They haven't been, so—" and she shrugged her shoulders, "there's not much point in discussing it, is there?"

He did not reply. Indeed, Eleanor was doubtful whether he heard much of what she had said for he was clearly lost in thought—and judging by his expression, not very pleasant ones at that.

She waited in silence, watching the clear flame from the logs as it leapt and flickered. Suddenly he spoke.

"I don't like it!" he said violently.

"Don't like what?" Eleanor asked uncomprehendingly.

"This whole set-up!" he explained, his hands moving in a comprehensive movement. "But principally, the position Mrs. Chalfont's offer has put both you and us into. I feel you're being forced into making the decision you have—and that we are at least partly responsible for that! After all, it appears to have been pretty common knowledge that we wanted to have an interest in Chalfont's. And now she's offered what could be the thin end of the wedge—"

"Yes, I suppose it could," Eleanor said indifferently. "But it really needn't worry you, because it fits in perfectly with my plans."

"Which are?"

Eleanor shrugged her shoulders.

"Of considerable interest to me, but very boring to other people. My mother is marrying again—an American. And I'm going to America with them."

"Permanently?" Jervis asked in a voice which gave no indication whether it was genuine interest or mere curiosity which prompted the question.

"Really, we've hardly discussed that yet," Eleanor replied casually. "But certainly for a good long time."

"I see."

She could not see his face, for he had bent forward to readjust a log that was in danger of falling.

"In that case, of course I can appreciate your reason for wanting to sell out," he commented. "So the situation is that I can tell my father that you are, in principle, giving us the first offer of a take-over bid?"

"Yes," Eleanor said firmly.

Jervis stood up.

"We'll let you know as soon as possible." He hesitated. "By the way, you realise that before we can make a definite offer we will have to have a more detailed knowledge of the state of your firm's finances."

"Naturally," Eleanor agreed coolly.

Again he hesitated.

"That will, of course, mean getting accountants, actuaries and solicitors on to the job. But before that, would you agree to a more informal inspection of your works and your books?"

"By you, personally?" Eleanor asked swiftly.

"Yes."

Now it was Eleanor's turn to hesitate. Of course Stapleton's would want to know just what they were letting themselves into, but this, she felt, was rather an odd way to go about gaining the information they wanted. It put them in a very strong bargaining position, whereas she—

Suddenly she capitulated. What did it matter? Quite apart from the works, Uncle Simon had left her comfortably off—whether she screwed the last penny out of Jervis and his father didn't matter to that degree. And she was so desperately tired—

"Very well," she agreed listlessly.

*　　　*　　　*

As Eleanor had thought more than likely, when Mr. Franklin heard of the arrangement she had made with Jervis, he didn't approve. He was also obviously put out that she had not consulted him before taking such a step.

"Yes, I know just what you mean, Mr. Franklin," she told him. "I'm giving them an opportunity, before they're really committed in any way, of finding out far more about our affairs than we can possibly know about theirs. Which could mean that they offer too low a price. But I don't think they will, you know. And in any case, I don't really care if they do. And after all, it is strictly my business, isn't it? I mean, I shall be the only one to suffer, won't I?"

"That may well be," Mr. Franklin said huffily. "But all this informality—"

"But that's just the point," Eleanor interrupted. "Formality means that everything takes a long time. Informality cuts corners, and that's what I want. Don't you understand, Mr. Franklin, that the sooner I can be free of this, the better pleased I shall be. And," she added significantly, "I don't think it's really strange that

I should feel like that in the circumstances, do you?"

And, however reluctantly, Mr. Franklin had to admit that there was a lot in what she said.

*   *   *

That Jervis would be thorough in the task he had undertaken, Eleanor had never doubted. What she had not realised was that he would make such a demand on her time.

For a fortnight after Jervis and his father had formally agreed with Eleanor that if terms could be agreed upon, they would take over Chalfont's completely, including Kingsworthy House, Jervis had spent four or five hours every day working in the room which Eleanor had used as Simon's secretary.

And seldom a day passed when he didn't ask Eleanor for information which meant breaking off from her own work to plough through figures and correspondence with him until he was satisfied that he fully understood their significance. He was very apologetic about it, however.

"I'm afraid I'm being a terrible nuisance to you," he said ruefully. "But it's the sort of job where one must be thorough or one might as well not do it at all."

Eleanor could have told him that she had been pleasantly surprised and genuinely impressed by the integrity and impartiality which he had brought to the task he had undertaken. Had she not known to the contrary, it would have been easy to imagine that he was a disinterested third party, so fairly did he balance the claims of both firms.

Just what prevented her from telling him this she could not clearly have defined, but in general terms she thought it was something to do with the fact that though the close companionship into which they were thrown was entirely due to the claims of business, none the less, Jervis was slowly emerging as a real person—and a likeable one at that. More than once she was reminded of what Jervis himself had said—if things had been different, they might have been good friends. But that, of course, was out of the question. Not only was she going to America, but once this transaction was completed, even if she had remained in England, their paths would have been unlikely to cross.

So she contented herself with saying that it was quite all right. She appreciated how he felt about it, and added :

"But I must warn you, I shall be going up to London for two days next week. My mother, as I told you, is getting married."

"Yes, I remember," Jervis nodded as he stirred the cup of very good coffee over which they had a brief morning break. "Which two days?"

"Wednesday and Thursday," Eleanor told him.

"And then?" he asked. "I mean, when will you be going to America?"

"Oh, not for another three weeks after that," Eleanor explained. "Mother and Mr. Elliot are doing a tour of England and Scotland for their honeymoon. Then they'll be coming to Kingsworthy House for a few days and then we'll go off together."

"Flying?" Jervis asked casually.

Eleanor laughed.

"No. Mother says she's got so much luggage they'd have to charter a good-sized plane to take it. We're sailing from Southampton about the middle of next month."

"Should be an extremely interesting and enjoyable experience," Jervis commented, setting down his cup. "I quite envy you. Now, about that export order you're waiting to have confirmed—"

And they were back to business again.

*   *   *

"And you're quite sure you're not heartbroken over Geoff?" Kitty asked anxiously—a very much younger, prettier, and certainly happier Kitty than Eleanor had ever seen before. By comparison, she herself felt dowdy and even elderly in the face of that gay sparkle.

"Quite sure, Mother," Eleanor said steadily. "And please, do believe that because though it's true, it's the sort of thing one simply can't prove. And I admit I found it difficult to believe myself—" And she shook her head as if it still puzzled her.

"Well, I don't, darling," Kitty declared firmly. "Where Geoff was concerned, you were living in a world of illusion left over from your childhood, and one day that was bound to fade. Geoff is a very nice boy, but to my way of thinking he's never quite grown up. That's why I grabbed the opportunity of suggesting that you should postpone your wedding. I hoped, even so late, you'd realise—"

Why, that was really just what Geoff himself had said, and Eleanor was ashamed of herself because she had never before realised that her mother had so much penetration and understanding.

Kitty, deep in her own thoughts, did not appear to recognise any particular significance of her remark which saved Eleanor an awkward exclamation. None the less, her next comment was perhaps even more disconcerting.

"You know, darling," she said reflectively, "they do say that the surest thing to make one forget an unhappy love affair is to fall in love with someone else. I suppose—?" She left the sentence unfinished, but her raised eyebrows were eloquent.

Eleanor laughed.

"Good gracious, no!" she declared, and then, not at all sure that she had convinced her mother, she sought to distract her by saying lightly: "Not but what I've had two proposals—of a sort!"

"Of a sort?" Kitty repeated suspiciously. "You surely don't mean—"

"Oh, nothing improper, darling," Eleanor assured her hurriedly. "Most respectable. And both from the same man—Jervis Stapleton!"

"Jervis Stapleton?" Kitty's eyes nearly popped out of her head. "Eleanor, I don't believe it!"

"It's true," Eleanor told her, "but don't imagine there was anything of a grand romance about it. It was simply that he pointed out that if we were to get married, many of our business problems would vanish. Which was true, of course," she added reflectively.

"You mean to say you're going to—" Kitty stopped short, completely out of her depth.

"Oh, good gracious, no!" Eleanor now heartily wishing that she'd never introduced the topic, spoke more emphatically than she realised. "We agreed that convenient though it might be, one really would have to be in love before thinking of marriage. So that was that. And in any case, now that Stapleton's are taking us over, there wouldn't be any point in it, would there?"

"No, I suppose not," Kitty agreed absently, and then, brightening up as the door opened: "Oh, here's Cranmer at last! Cranmer darling, this is my girl!"

*   *   *

Eleanor *did* like Cranmer Elliot. It would have been difficult not to, for not only was he very intelligent, good-looking in a masculine way and kindly, but he was so evidently the right man for Kitty. Nor was that only because he gave her a feeling of security which was not altogether due to the fact that he was a rich man. Even in the comparatively short time that they had known one another, he had contrived to help Kitty develop into a very much nicer person than she had been before. And that did not surprise Eleanor. Her prospective stepfather had the supreme gift of putting people at their ease so that they expanded in his company as naturally as flowers in the sunshine. Very soon Eleanor discovered what the secret of his gift was. He was genuinely interested in his fellow beings.

He was interested in Eleanor and she found herself telling him in far greater detail than she had anyone else just what had happened since Simon's death. Only one thing she kept silent about—her broken engagement. And though, presumably, Kitty had told him about this, he made no reference to it. Simply, when she had finished her story, he had nodded understandingly.

"Yes, I'd say you were right to get out," he told her. "Not only because you'd been forced into a position you never sought without your consent, but because, as you yourself say, it wasn't your line of country. You'd never have been happy as a career woman—and in my opinion, only a very few women are. And even then, I wouldn't say but what they miss the best things in life! Well, honey, you've had a pretty bad time, but now that's all but over. Your mother and I plan to give you the best time ever once we get back to the States, so you look forward to that, and forget all the rest!"

They went to the theatre that night—not, fortunately, one to which Eleanor and Geoff had planned to go, for that might perhaps have stirred memories that were best left to fade. Eleanor enjoyed herself considerably, especially after the show when they went to a night club. There they met several junior Embassy officials and Eleanor was almost danced off her feet.

"But nothing, darling, to what it's going to be back in New York!" Kitty declared joyously.

The wedding was the next morning. It was very quiet, attended only by Eleanor and the two friends on whose yacht the bride and bridegroom met. After the ceremony there was a wedding lunch at the hotel and then the new Mrs. Elliot and her husband went off in his huge chauffeur-driven car on their tour. Eleanor, after having gratefully refused Stephanie's invitation to stay on a few days in London as their guest, caught the train for Kingswell which would get her there in the late afternoon.

By now, though the sun had been obliging enough to shine during the wedding, a fine drizzle was now coming down and there was a chill in the air. Eleanor shivered a little in the pretty summer outfit she had chosen for the wedding—and not only because the temperature had dropped considerably. Of course she hadn't been so mean as to envy her mother, but all the same, Kitty's obvious happiness and above all the companionship she could look forward to served to remind Eleanor of her own loneliness. When she left England, no one would really mind. Indeed, to some people, it might even be a relief that she was going. To Celia and Geoff it would certainly come as release from any feeling of guilt. And the Stapletons, no doubt, would be quite glad to have her out of the neighbourhood.

But for the moment those things were of secondary importance. It was the thought of going to an empty, probably chilly house where there would be no one to welcome her, no one who would be in the least interested in what she had been doing during the last two days.

But it had to be faced. When the train drew into Kingswell station she got briskly out of her compartment, and started walking along the platform carrying her case.

"Allow me!" said a familiar voice, and she gave a little gasp as Jervis took her case from her.

"Sorry if I startled you!" he apologised. "You were miles away, weren't you?"

"Not really," Eleanor confessed. "It was just—I was funking going home to an empty house, and trying to pretend I didn't mind!"

"But you're not going to," Jervis said quietly. "I've got the car here and I'm going to run you to Kingsworthy House—if I may?"

"Of course you may!" Eleanor said warmly, that horrible sense of bleakness vanishing in a flash. And then, diffidently: "I suppose you wouldn't like to stay and share a meal with me? I'm afraid it will be rather a scratch affair, but I think we could rise to bacon and eggs."

"And what could be better?" Jervis asked gaily as he opened the car door and helped her in.

It was half-past ten before he left the West Pavilion. The meal had been a resounding success and so had the coffee which Jervis undertook to brew. After that they simply sat and talked—about anything that came into their minds. Anything, that is, except business—and anything which might have been described as dealing with personal relationships.

And then, quite suddenly, silence fell on both of them —a silence which seemed to grow in intensity, and which neither of them seemed capable of breaking.

Not that Eleanor wanted to do so. It was heaven just to sit here, warm and fed, and strangely at peace. She had entirely lost that terrible sense of loneliness and emptiness. Instead, life seemed to be fuller and richer than it had ever been before.

And then into her mind flashed dazzling comprehension. The reason for her happy contentment was simply that Jervis was here with her.

And that, she knew, meant only one thing. All unconsciously, during these last few weeks, she had learned to love Jervis.

It may have been that she made a slight movement or perhaps some little sound. Or could it have been that Jervis read her thoughts? Whatever the cause, he started suddenly, glanced at his watch and stood up abruptly.

"My dear girl, you should have reminded me of the time!" he remarked. "I was so comfortable, I'm afraid I forgot all about it! But you must be tired——"

"Only comfortably so," Eleanor contrived to speak, as she thought, quite naturally and easily, but she saw that Jervis looked at her with sudden intensity, and her eyes dropped from his. Supposing he had guessed—and was, of course, embarrassed since, of course, he didn't feel like that about her!

And if she had wanted any confirmation of that, she had it in the way in which he made his hurried farewell and almost dashed from the house.

Nor, in the weeks that followed, did they ever get on to what might in any way be called friendly terms. Jervis was briskly businesslike, and sheer pride and self-respect compelled Eleanor to follow his lead.

Even when, on the eve of her departure, they signed the very last of the documents which finally transferred all her interests in Chalfont's to Stapleton's, his manner did not change. Efficient, brisk, impersonal—he did, in fact, with her a pleasant trip and an enjoyable holiday, but then he really had little choice but to do so.

"Oh, I'm sure I shall," she heard herself say in a bright, brittle voice. "I'm looking forward to it tremendously."

Briefly an expression which she couldn't interpret flickered over his face, but there was no change in his voice as he said lightly:

"In that case, I hope it more than comes up to your expectations!"

*   *   *

It was not until the liner was well out to sea that Eleanor came on deck. She had not wanted to see or hear the farewells between passengers and their friends who had thought it worth while to come and

see them off. It hurt too much to know that no one cared
sufficiently to want to be with her until the very last
moment. Nor did she want to see the coastline gradually fade from sight. So she had done her own unpacking, which had been quite a long job because Kitty had
insisted on buying her more clothes than she had ever
before possessed in all her life. Then she lent her mother
a hand with her unpacking and finally, when really
there was no excuse to put it off any longer, she sought
out this quiet little nook which, so far, she had to herself.
It was well forward, and deliberately she gazed in a
westerly direction, refusing to think of anything except
that she was going to start a new life in a new country
in circumstances which promised to be both enjoyable
and exciting—if only she was sensible.

"So do stop pitying yourself and just remember that
most people would give their eye-teeth to be in your shoes,
my girl," she told herself sternly. "All you've got to do is
turn yourself into a new person to match. It ought not
to be difficult—I hope," she finished less valiantly, but
she would not let herself mop up the tears that sprang
to her eyes. That would have been a confession of failure
that she was afraid to make.

She stayed there quite a long time, fascinated by the
glint of sunshine on the restless sea that so matched her
own mood.

Would she ever be able to forget? Oh, not just the
unhappiness and anxiety of the last few months. All
that had faded into insignificance in the light of her
incredible discovery that she loved Jervis. Not in that
blind, adoring way in which she had loved Geoff. Her
mother had been right in saying that that was something
left over from her childhood. This was something much
deeper and more mature. Something which, had it been
fulfilled would have meant a lifetime of companionship
and shared experiences. But it would never be more than
just a dream because Jervis, of course, just wasn't interested. In all probability, particularly as she was determined never to go back to Kingswell, she would never
see him again—

"So this is where you've got," said a slightly aggrieved

voice. "Do you know, I've ransacked the ship to find you!"

It couldn't be true! It must be her imagination! Jervis was miles away, still on dry land—Eleanor stood very still, lest any movement might dissolve this waking dream.

He was standing directly behind her and now he stretched out a hand and gripped the rail on either side of her so that she was a prisoner.

"Eleanor?" There was a question in his voice, but though her heart beat wildly, she dared not answer it.

"But—but why are you here?" she asked through dry lips without turning her head.

"Because I love you," Jervis said simply, and then, wryly: "As I could have told you long since, but for one thing."

"Me being engaged to Geoff?" Eleanor suggested, oddly anxious, now that she had heard him say that, not to grab too heedlessly at her happiness. This was something worth waiting for—and there were still explanations to be made.

"No, darling, not that. Somehow, to me, that never did ring true—and I don't think it was just a question of wishful thinking—?"

"No, it wasn't," she answered gravely. "And you weren't the only people who felt that. Oh, I don't mean the uncles. They wanted to believe it. But Mother and Aunt Helen—that was different. They were really concerned for me."

"And you?"

"I never stopped to think. Geoff and I had always been such good friends. And from when I was quite little, he'd always seemed so wonderful. Just being with him made me happy. And yet when I knew how he felt about Celia, I didn't feel surprised or particularly hurt. Only—frightfully empty. But never mind that. If it wasn't Geoff, what was it that kept you from telling me?"

"Quite a lot of things," Jervis said ruefully. "But all really stemming from the enmity between your family and mine. At every turn, that baulked me. You'd been taught to mistrust any Stapleton. Yet every now

ind then I thought perhaps you were beginning to believe that perhaps I wasn't quite as black as I'd been
painted. Then no sooner had I dared to let myself hope
than something cropped up that sent me back to square
one. And I was never sure if that was chance—or
whether it was deliberate contriving on someone's part.
Which do you think it was?"

"I—I don't want to think about it, please, Jervis. It's
over and done with—we're free of it all—"

"Are we?" Jervis asked urgently. "You honestly believe that?"

"Yes, I do," Eleanor said positively. "More than ever
think what I said to you before is true—it's terrible,
but Uncle Edgar's death has set a good many people
free, including me. And—" she hesitated momentarily—
"you?"

"Yes," Jervis replied unhesitatingly. "Particularly as,
because of that, the obstacles which kept me from telling you I loved you have gone. Not but what I had
myself to blame partly for that. If I'd not been such a
fool as to say that all our troubles would vanish into
thin air if we were to get married, I wouldn't have had
to wait until you could know for certain that I've no
ulterior motive in asking you to do just that! And how
I managed to hold my tongue, I'll never know! There
were times—one in particular. That day I met you when
you came back after your mother's wedding—that was
the third train I'd met, by the way—you looked so little
and lost, I wanted to sweep you into my arms and com-
ort you. In the end I ran away because I couldn't trust
myself to keep quiet! I was so desperately scared you'd
turn round and tell me again that people don't get
married just to solve business problems."

"Well, they don't, do they?" Eleanor said pensively.
I still feel that, Jervis."

"In that case—" he spoke lightly, but she saw that
his grip on the rail tightened until his knuckles were
white, "I must warn you, Miss Chalfont, that for the
remainder of our voyage, I intend to pay court to you
on every occasion with such empressment that by the
time we sight the Statue of Liberty, it will be no fault

of mine if you haven't fallen a complete victim to my charms!"

"And if I don't?" she spoke gravely, but there was a sparkle in her eyes that she was not ready for him to see yet.

"If you don't—" his voice harshened. "Then, my dear, we'll say goodbye, and I won't worry you again. That's a promise so you needn't be afraid to give me my chance."

"No, I needn't, need I?" Eleanor agreed. "But there is just one thing—"

Jervis waited in silence, a muscle twitching at the corner of his mouth.

"It will take us four or five days to get to New York, won't it?" she said reflectively.

"Yes," he confirmed curtly, his heart sinking.

"But you told me once, that day when we picnicked together, that a weekend—two or three days at the most —was quite long enough for *anybody* to know whether they were in love or not," she reminded him with deceptive demureness. "Have you changed your mind about that?"

With a wordless exclamation he turned her about and gazed with incredulous delight into her flushed, happy face. Her lips were smiling, and in her eyes was a promise.

He knew what he had not dared to hope—that he didn't have to wait any longer for the answer he so longed to hear from her.

Perhaps, by and by, there would have to be more explanations, but for the time being they were unimportant. Only one thing mattered. Against all odds, they had found one another.

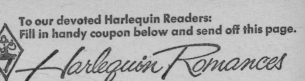

To our devoted Harlequin Readers:
Fill in handy coupon below and send off this page.

TITLES STILL IN PRINT

51465   DAMSEL IN GREEN, B. Neels

51466   RETURN TO SPRING, J. Macleod

51467   BEYOND THE SWEET WATERS, A. Hampson

51468   YESTERDAY, TODAY AND TOMORROW, J. Dunbar

51469   TO THE HIGHEST BIDDER, H. Pressley

51470   KING COUNTRY, M. Way

51471   WHEN BIRDS DO SING, F. Kidd

51472   BELOVED CASTAWAY, V. Winspear

51473   SILENT HEART, L. Ellis

51474   MY SISTER CELIA, M. Burchell

51475   THE VERMILION GATEWAY, B. Dell

51476   BELIEVE IN TOMORROW, N. Asquith

51477   THE LAND OF THE LOTUS EATERS, I. Chace

51478   EVE'S OWN EDEN, K. Mutch

51479   THE SCENTED HILLS, R. Lane

51480   THE LINDEN LEAF, J. Arbor

~~~~~~~~~~~~~~~~~~~~~~~~~~~~~~~~~

Harlequin Books, Dept. Z

Simon & Schuster, Inc., 11 West 39th St.
New York, N.Y. 10018

☐ Please send me information about Harlequin Romance Subscribers Club.

Send me titles checked above. I enclose .50 per copy plus .15 per book for postage and handling.

Name ....

Address ....

City .... State .... Zip ....